In The Company Of Cows

Sequoyah Branham

Published by Sequoyah Branham, 2023.

IN THE COMPANY OF COWS

First edition. October 24, 2023.

ISBN: 979-8988190011

Written by Sequoyah Branham.

To my own personal Uncle Ian.

Brazos Davis

January 25, 1966 - June 3, 2022

Without you there would be no *In The Company Of Cows*.

Chapter 1

I shouldn't have washed my hair last night. My hat never will stay on in this wind.

I brace on the balls of my feet as a West Texas wind gust shoves me toward the pens north of the house. It grabs at the back of my wide-brimmed hat, and I push it farther down on my head.

If this dang wind doesn't stop blowing, we won't have to worry about needing rain. There won't be enough dirt left to grow grass in.

Half of Iraan's dirt blew through on a south wind the last three days, blasting everything with caliche, including the eleven Hereford heifers. Their red coats are tainted gray as they lie around chewing their cuds, looking more as though they are recovering from an all-you-can-eat buffet than about to calve.

Come on, girls, we have been without a new calf for a week and a half. It would be nice to walk out to a calf on the ground.

Two, four, six, eight head. I hop up on the fence to peek over the hay ring. Nine, ten, and... no eleven. I step around the edge of the fence, training my eyes for her. She's probably just hiding. After several steps, I spot her. In the corner, stretched out on her side, is #94. For an instant my feet are frozen to the ground before adrenaline takes over.

No time for gate latches. I leap over the fence. A low bawl from her sends a rock down to the pit of my stomach. She was bred by the neighbor's bull, and he is anything but small.

How did I miss the signs last check?

1

"Hey, sister." I ease up behind her. Two front feet stick out under her tail but don't move when a contraction overtakes her. Crap! Those feet are definitely supposed to be moving. Hopefully that baby's nose isn't already blue. I'm not losing another one to calving-itis.

Faster than a calf learns to stand, I run to the barn. *Lord, I could use some help. Keep the little feller alive, please.* In the barn I shed my jean jacket, roll up my sleeves, and load down my arms. Two pairs of chains and a cow halter with an old nylon rope tied to the end of it will have to do the job. *You definitely should have gone to town and gotten more cable to fix the calf puller, Nora. It'd come in handy right about now.*

Standing behind the heifer, I drop a loop around her nose. She starts to rise, but I get a knee in her neck before she gets up. *Don't call my bluff, sister, 'cause you can pitch me off here in half a second.*

My breath comes in quick puffs. *Let's see if I can get an eye poked out.* I lean up and yank the halter over her horns and behind her ears. Score! Gripping the coiled rope, I jump off her neck and take off for the nearest three-inch pipe. Two wraps and a quick release knot, now we get to work.

The chain is cool against my sweaty palms as I put a half hitch around each front leg of the calf. *Okay, hang in there, bud.* I take the metal handles in both hands, plant my heels in the powdery dirt, and gradually lean back against the chains. *Come on.*

The momma-to-be bellers as a contraction overtakes her, and I pull harder. "There you go, come on," I mumble.

The calf slides forward. I step back. A dark gray nose pokes out into the air, its edges tainted with hints of blue. My right hand claws the slimy sack away from the calf's nostrils. "Breathe, baby, breathe."

Suddenly, it's not a hereford heifer that bawls, but a curly-headed smokey that I had raised on a bottle. *Don't go there. It's not dead yet.* "Are you, buddy?"

One more pull and the help of nature's contraction slides the rest of the calf's body onto the bare ground. Sliding my arm around its middle, I drape it over its mother's belly, head down. When I tickle in its nostril, no air meets my finger.

"Breathe." The word comes in a pant.

One hand on top of the other, I pump against its ribs. After a couple times I step back. Unless I'm imagining things, its belly is rising. I ease around the front of #94 and tug at the halter rope. It pops loose, and she hums to the calf, head craned around. Her sandpaper tongue slides down the calf's back, and its ear twitches. My lungs hold breath hostage and my eyes flick from its belly to its ear and then to those deep brown eyes that blink at the morning light.

"Just needed Momma's touch." The cracks in my lips split open from how far they are spread in a grin.

I soak it all in for a moment before stripping the chains from the calf, easing it down in front of Momma, and taking a peek between its legs. Another bull calf for Wade's bottom dollar!

Hair falls into my eye, and I brush it away with an afterbirth-sticky hand, undoubtedly smearing dirt, hay, and slime across my forehead. The rhythm of that sandpaper tongue licking away the remains of the womb brings as much life to my heart as it does to the calf's body.

Blood and mucus and dirt dry on my arms as I watch the little fella try his wobbly legs. They crater under him, and his momma hums softly to him, nudging his hip. He tries a couple more times before he teeters on all fours and takes a shaky step toward his momma's flank. I wrap my arms around myself and squeak in satisfaction. Some moments never get old, even after three straight years of them.

At the water trough I plunge my arms in and work my fingers over each link of the chain. A breeze blows as I pull my arms out, sending a shiver down my back before I dip them in again. This time I scrub at the mess on my skin.

After I've put the chains and halter away, I roll down my sleeves and slip back into my jean jacket. I hug it tightly against myself and look on at the cow-calf pair. The bull calf has its nose in #94's flank, tail wagging with satisfaction.

"Thank you, Lord." I breathe out a sigh. It is always refreshing when the food part of their brain works right off the bat.

The sun casts an orange and pink hue behind the pair, making it picture-perfect. Not that I have my phone on me to take it. Or have someone to share it with. I capture it in my mind and then turn back to the barn.

As I emerge with a bucket of oats, a soft nicker floats my way. I look up into three varying shades of soft red noses. "Good morning, boys." My shoulders rise, and the sweet smell of horses fills my lungs, along with half a horse's worth of hair.

Who needs friends? I've got all the friends I need right here. They never interrupt me when I talk, but they don't care if I never say a word either. "Isn't that right, Dune?" I push the sorrel over and pour the oats down the length of the trough.

***

After a cup of coffee and a couple pieces of bacon, I slide my feet into the worn boots that always carry my spurs. All three of my geldings' heads pop up as I approach the pens, but they don't move from under the mesquite by the water trough. I grab the hackamore off the front of a peg in the barn before slipping through their gate.

Cante, my three-year-old giant scaredy cat, blows heavily through his nostrils but lets me slide the rawhide bosal over his nose. A greasewood branch waves as he follows me through the gate, and he spins out, making the reins tight. I shake my head. "Can't give you a day off, can I?"

He runs a good bluff of being a bad one, but really he's scared of his own shadow. I thought a name like Cante would make him brave, but so far it hasn't. He's lived up to it and is full of heart, though.

Standing in front of the barn, I pass a hand under his belly, and his skin twitches. I smirk. If he were a deadhead, it wouldn't be any fun. As I swing my saddle over his back, the off-side stirrup slaps his side. He arcs his body towards me but runs into my outstretched hand and freezes with a snort.

"Golly," I mumble, eyeing his back feet as I reach under him for the cinch. His ear cocks towards me, but he doesn't move again.

I pull my tan shotgun leggins on and debate about shedding my jacket. The sun is well up in the sky, but the breeze still has a little bite to it. Eh, I can always tie it on behind the cantle in an hour or so when I'm nice and toasty.

Cante follows me through several gates into the west pasture. I take the cinch up a couple holes and send him into a trot around me. After a couple circles, his stride smooths out. One more time I take the cinch up, then walk him a few steps and gather a handful of mane in one hand with the cotton reins. My right hand barely can finger the saddlehorn. Cante watches me and steps his back end around just as I'm about to jump and catch the stirrup. I eye him back and take up on the left rein. One jump and I slide the toe of my left foot into the wooden U, propelling myself into the seat. Cante lets out a big breath.

"That a'boy." I lean down and pat his neck.

His trot is stiff, and I can feel the slightest swell in his back, but when I smooch him into a lope, he relaxes quickly. I let him have at it for a quarter mile or so before reining him in to a trot. My gaze swivels from side to side, and I cringe. Prickly pear, tasajillo, cholla, greasewood, blackbrush, and two blades of grass in the very middle of a tasajillo bush. We should have moved these girls off this country a year ago.

Suddenly, Cante's stride gets stiff, and his neck shrinks six inches. Up ahead a little bunch of red bodies sticks out amongst the dull tannish-gray landscape. The heifer closest to us raises its head just as I sit deeper in my saddle, giving Cante the slightest cue to slow to a walk. The bovine and equine give one another an equally curious stare for a long moment before the heifer steps into the middle of her friends and Cante's neck relaxes back to normal. I start counting to the tune of mesquite leaves being ground between my horse's teeth.

Eleven head. I direct Cante through the middle of them. The heifers cluster around us. Typical heifers, not about to cooperate and let me get a good look. I rest my hand on top of the saddlehorn and stare at them with raised eyebrows. "Really, girls? We go through this every morning."

At least there aren't any calves hanging halfway out the back end of any of them. I shrug out of my jacket and tie it on my saddle before trying again to step around behind the girls. This time I get a good enough look to see none of them are starting a bag yet. They've got time.

"Thanks, girls," I call and point Cante toward a thicket in the middle of the pasture. The sad part is this trap is the least brushy one we have.

In the middle of the thicket, fifteen head are scattered. Getting Cante through it to push them out and get a good look is like riding four ping-pong balls going in five directions. His sporadic dodging of poky and non-poky bushes alike jostles me around the saddle and into the few limbs that are actually tall enough to reach my head.

He stops, a two-foot-tall mesquite in his path. Arching away from it, he tries to turn around. *Sorry bud, there's a bigger tree there.* I touch his sides with my spurs. He puts his head under a floppy branch, takes it out, and slips it back under again. I apply more pressure with my spurs. I feel his hind end gather up under me. One, two, three, he launches into an overly dramatic jump, and out the other side we go. The heifers scatter, trotting off fifteen feet or so before turning to face us.

"See, bud, you didn't get eaten in there." I have to chuckle a little. Poor guy still hasn't figured out how to be a brush pony.

We make several circles around the heifers before I am satisfied. Two are getting floppy in the back end. I'll take them to the pens to join the waiting game.

Farther down the trail we run into four more head. A ball of lead instantly forms in my belly. One heifer by herself is practically a death sentence. *Please, don't let it be.* Two crises in one morning is bad for the heart.

Focus.

I look the four over more closely. They don't look any more bred than last time I saw them, but if possible, they look more in need of feed than before.

I scan the pasture as if expecting the last heifer to come walking up. The greasewood is hardly tall enough to hide a dead cow, let alone a live one. Leaning forward and poking Cante with my spurs, I send him into the next brush thicket. Catclaw grabs at my shirt but doesn't rip it. Cante balks at the first tasajillo bush, and I flick the end of a rein on his rump. We do not have time for this.

He jumps another bush, and almost before he lands I am pulling one rein back to my hip. Cante stops, then sees the carcass and skids to the side and snorts. My shoulders fall. So much for hurrying.

Calving-itis. I shake my head and try not to breathe too deeply. This is what I'm here for; I'm supposed to keep this from happening. I chew on my bottom lip and then hit the saddlehorn with my fist.

Dang it! Why can't I be everywhere at once? It's sure not the first time, and it won't be the last. I sigh and turn Cante away. My feelings are so used to being stuffed in envelopes, they don't even hesitate. I set fire to the envelope as the smell floats away.

As Pawpaw always said, if you're going to have livestock, you're going to have dead stock.

The two I need to take back to the house are around the remains of three hay bales I put out four or five days ago. "Damn it." The curse slips out under my breath before I even register it. These cattle need grass and lots of it. Even if I had been there to help that heifer, they are all so weak she might not have made it anyway.

Quietly, I ease the two away from their friends, working side to side behind them until they line out down the trail. Cante's head swings in time with his long stride before the pens come into sight and I disturb his peaceful gait.

As we ease around the front of the heifers to the gate, wind sends a swirl of hay and manure flakes into my face. The heifers are up milling around but aren't near the gate as I tie it back. I keep one eye on the gate over my shoulder as I trot back to where the two new hostages have stopped in the middle of the trail. The hostages bawl and pick up a trot all the way into the middle of their friends.

I step to the ground and notice the gray Dodge sitting in the road by the barn. Pulling the gate around, I spot Wade leaning up against the fence watching the heavies. No wonder they were milling. My hands get the itch to hide, and my mind scrambles for all the things I'm supposed to do and say.

"Morning, boss," I call, thankful my hands have the pickin' string to play with.

He holds the second gate open for me, and I lead Cante out in front of his pickup. "I'm glad I caught you! When you didn't answer my call, I thought you might already be halfway to Big Lake on him." He nods toward my sweaty gelding.

"Not yet." I shake his stubby hand, then my thumb finds the string of my leggins to hang from.

Wade leans against the gate, his classic Hawaiian shirt rippling around his paunch of a gut. Not the image of a rancher, but then most that know him think of Wade as a farmer with cattle rather than a rancher. "How many you got left to calve?"

"Fourteen up here now. Twenty-eight left to bring up." I move a rock with the toe of my boot. A very unusually round rock, no less. "Found one laid out in the brush this morning. Didn't make it."

He nods, his hand dropping to his side. A weathered smile lifts the corner of his lips ever so slightly. "They might finish up before we have to move them off of here yet."

For the first time, I spare a glance at his eyes. What is that look? Heaviness? Hopelessness? "Have you found a place, then?"

"No." He looks up at me, and my eyes dart away. "I'm not going to lie to you, Nora, there's not a darn thing turning up. There doesn't seem to be a blade of grass trying to grow around here. We can't keep feeding the cattle everything they get." He wets his lips and looks down. "Selling out is sure looking like the only way to go."

No! I scream in my head. dadgummit, it's not the only way. It can't be.

I look over the heifers. What would a sunrise be without their silhouettes in it? "What if you have help finding a lease?"

His gaze swings around to me, and I have to bolt my feet to the ground to keep them from following my brain that just ran away. "What do you have in mind?"

"My Uncle Ian is in ranch real estate. Surely he knows someone somewhere that just wants to lease their land for a while."

Just because he and Dad haven't ever been close doesn't mean he won't do me a favor, right?

Wade arches one eyebrow and then the other. He looks back at the heifers. "I don't see how it'd hurt anything. Give him a call and let me know what you find out." He claps his hand against my shoulder and walks around the front of his pickup. "I'm on my way to meet James at headquarters. Holler at you later!"

I raise my hand in a half-hearted wave as he makes the circle and leaves a cloud of dust for me to breathe in. What on earth did I just volunteer myself for? There's a reason my phone stays in the house and is hardly worth the forty dollars I pay for service every month. I don't like using it. Not even to talk to Wade or James about cattle, and certainly not to an uncle I've never had more than a two-second conversation with.

But it's not just the heifers on the line now. If this doesn't go well, I can kiss ever having a relationship with my idol of an uncle goodbye forever.

Chapter 2

One, two, three, spin on heels, one, two, three.

My thumb hovers over the green circle on my ancient iPhone. Three letters stare me down from the top of the screen. 'Ian.' I sigh, and my arm falls against my thigh, sending a puff of powdery white dirt from my jeans. On the table, a plate of ground beef and beans sits cold. Usually it is my favorite to scoop up in a tortilla chip and chow down on, but not with this phone call looming over my head.

In. Out. The tightness in my chest doesn't go out with the breath.

Just get the phone call over with. The worst he can say is no. I close my eyes and try to steady the runaway heart in my chest. *But if he does say no...*

The trilling rings send my heart into a full stampede, one that can't be turned into a mill.

Five rings. Now ten. How many times does a phone have to ring before the voicemail comes on?

"This is Ian Kelly. Sorry I missed—"

I jerk the phone from my ear, stab the red circle, and let the device clatter onto the wooden table. One of the riders just got trampled trying to mill my heart's stampede.

Like Cante eyeing something new, I eye the phone on the table. I'll just have to figure out a different way to find a lease.

I lift my hand, and it shakes like a leaf in the wind. Fresh air, that's what I need.

With the same leaflike hands, I fumble through the console of the old ranch pickup for my wallet. Under several inches of receipts and a couple calendar books, I feel it. I stuff it in the cubby hole under the radio. The pickup spits and sputters before it gets into a rhythm and sounds half-right. Once-a-week excursions aren't always enough to keep the old thing on the straight and narrow.

As the wheels start turning, taking me away from the house with the cellular device in it, I don't look in the mirrors. Seeing dust boil up behind me isn't comforting.

From the tidbits I had gotten from my mom, who keeps up with Ian's wife, Ian has been trying to scale down the real estate business and increase his cattle numbers. His niece's sob story must be the last thing he wants to hear. Not to mention he doesn't have time for it. Anyone who has livestock knows it takes all the time you have and a little that you don't.

Stupid. It was a stupid idea. I'll just take the humiliation of telling Wade it won't work out.

But something has to.

At the blinking light in the middle of town, I wait for a couple cars to turn before doing it myself. I do a U-turn across the street and back up against the loading dock at the feed store. Pablo stands on the edge of the dock and waves me back.

"Afternoon, Miss Nora. You didn't bring any rain with you."

"Not today." I sigh but smile at the familiar exchange that started years ago. Not many remember the last time it rained enough to talk about. "A pallet of protein tubs, please, sir."

"Yes, ma'am!"

I stroll to the open-fronted store, and paste on a smile. A couple walks out and I nod to them. Is it only guys that are supposed to nod like that? Oh, well.

"Nora! What are you after today?" Sam hollers when I'm still a couple yards from the counter.

I lean up against the counter with a little smile. "Another pallet of tubs. And you better go ahead and write me down for a truckload of hay."

All cheer drains from the older man's face. "Still ain't found nowhere to go?"

I shake my head and read the Ace Reid cartoons that hang behind Sam's head, for the millionth time.

"Ain't nothing been talked about around here, or I'd of done called Wade. It's been a year since I sold all but my feeder steer, and my place still doesn't have more than ten blades of grass." He rips the ticket out of the book and slides it to me.

My heart sinks. Rain. It takes rain for this country to come back, but are there even going to be any roots for the grass to come back from?

"Your uncle Ian says he can't count how many times he's been offered heifers to buy. Seems like the last ones are selling out."

Ian. The name doesn't come up to me more than once a month, but the one day I couldn't hear anything more disturbing is the day I hear it. "I'm afraid that'll be us next."

"Nah, something'll turn up. It always does." Sam looks around the building. "It's times like these that make me thankful for this place."

How could a man who probably doesn't get paid much more than minimum wage prefer nine hours of confinement over breathing fresh air, even if the air is tainted with manure? Maybe if Sam owned this place it would make more sense. He has been the face of it for so long most people don't know he isn't the owner.

"Thanks, Sam."

"You have a good day now, missy!"

Pablo is busy loading a flatbed, but I still wave to him as I drive away.

Two blocks down, at the grocery store, I cut the pickup engine. My pantry is beyond bare. It would probably prefer I went to Crane or at least Big Lake, but for now a couple bags of corn chips and another pound of cheese will have to do.

Not many people are in the store, which allows me to breathe a little easier. The fewer people, the less I have to worry about running into one of them and figuring out what to say. It doesn't take me long to zip around and grab the things I need. A few things I don't also end up in the brittle handheld basket, like a dozen flour tortillas and a bag of chocolate chips.

I spend two and a half minutes checking the mail before I'm on my way out of town. The oldies drown out the growl of tires on pavement and rattle of the worn-out engine, but not my nagging thoughts.

Ian has a voicemail. Why didn't I just leave a message the first time? Darn it. If I don't leave a message, I haven't actually tried my best to get ahold of him. It's either let the trilling drive me over the brink of insanity for a half minute or keep hoping against hope that land will fall into Wade's lap.

A reflection catches my attention and makes me sit up straighter. Maybe I should actually use my blinker since someone is behind me. I pull off to the side of the road as much as I dare without falling off into the bar ditch.

Gah-lee! There wasn't any oncoming traffic. You didn't have to almost take my bumper off. I eye my mirror for another ignorant sucker. When I look up, my turn is like right now. And James is sitting in the middle of it.

I slam on the brakes, but it does little. I press harder and pull hard to the right. Band-aids fix severed limbs, right? My lips part across my teeth, and I suck air in between them.

The tires grate on the gravel and stop spinning inches before my grill guard meets that of a red Chevy. My left eyelid can't close any harder. Man that was close!

I throw the gearshift into park and pant for breath. The window squeals as I roll it down.

"Didn't your daddy ever teach you what a steering wheel is for?" A self-amused chuckle vibrates from under the brim of a chocolate felt hat, bouncing off my traumatized nerves. He pushes his door open and unfolds himself from the single cab.

It takes a moment for the comment to register, and my head falls when it does. That's the thing about my dad—he didn't teach me much of anything. I look up into patiently amused eyes just like when we're sorting cattle. Steady Eddy James. I cough. "Sorry, I, uh, got precautioned, I mean, preoccupied by that pickup."

James rests his scarred hand on the door of my pickup. "He acted like his steering was out." His hand comes to rest lightly on my shoulder.

I should probably make eye contact now. I look up.

"Are you okay?"

I want to laugh, but don't have enough air in my lungs for that. Sounds like a teenager's dad, when he barely has passed teen years himself. "Yeah, yeah, I'm fine."

His eyes study me. "People just don't know how to give others space these days." His weight shifts from one foot to the other. "Wade told me there were some old telephone poles over here, but I didn't find any. I'll go to the dump at headquarters and scope out the old boards."

I look at his nose. It's such nice middle ground between dealing with eye contact and looking everywhere but at him. "I don't think there's any lumber out here."

"I'll find something." He slaps his palm against the window sill. "You need any help while I'm over here?"

My foot swivels over to the brake again. Nope, I'm good. I just need to go sit in a hole and convince my nerves to still function. "I don't think so."

His gaze bores holes in my skin.

Come on, James, now is not the time to play super detective.

"All right, I'll catch you later."

Out of the corner of my eye, I watch him fold his legs into the single cab and slam the door. The wheels start turning, and then he pokes his head out. "Next time scrape it. Maybe I can get a prettier grill guard then."

Yeah, let's not.

I pull the pickup into its usual spot at the end of the house. My arms feel like limp noodles, just like the first time I drove in a town with stoplights, with a trailer hooked on, no less. I hadn't had my license more than a month and only knew ranch roads. Three almost-wrecks is putting it mildly. It was that way with most things, though; just go do the thing, and I was left to hope I didn't die while figuring it out.

I sigh and grip the edge of my hat. Time to get the groceries in. They feel more like bags of sand than food as I plop them down on the counter. I don't bother putting them away.

The chip bag crinkles and then rips. My hand goes in empty, reemerging with half a dozen yellow corn chips. Ah, yes, this is what I've been missing the last week.

A chip crunches between my teeth, filling my eardrums, and I stare at my phone on the table. Heart attack or nagging guilt? I stuff another chip in my mouth and start for the device. It isn't just myself to let down: it's every heifer on this place, Wade, and the determination I have had since birth.

The chip sits dryly in my mouth. Half a glass of water almost doesn't wash it down. My heart starts racing again as I pick up the phone. A missed call and a text. My stomach seized but then let go. Both of them are from James and happened about an hour ago, before I talked to him.

I guzzle the rest of the water, lick my lips, and touch that three-letter name. Each ring echoes through my body. I spin the glass on the table. It clatters over and I snatch it before it can fall.

"This is Ian Kelly. Sorry I missed your call."

I jump, my heart thudding in my ears.

"Please leave your name, and number and I'll get back to you as soon as I can."

Deep breath. In and out. "Hi, Uncle Evan, uh, umm, sorry, Ian. This is Nora. I-uh-Nora Kelly. I'm trying to help my boss find some land to lease and thought maybe—"

Two beeps make me pull the phone away from my ear. The racing of my heart skids to a standstill. An incoming call has interrupted the voicemail. My tongue is cottony over my lips. And from none other than Ian Kelly.

Frosted potato flakes! What are words?

Chapter 3

Three options flash at the bottom of the screen. I blink in return. Two beeps, pause, two beeps.

End and accept. Decline. Hold and accept.

My thought process stands still. What do these options mean?

My finger hovers over the middle option, then the third. Ah, that's not what I want. I touch the first one, and it reignites the racing of my heart. I swallow back the thick saliva in my mouth. "H-hello?"

"Hey, Nora. It's good to hear from you."

I shove my free hand in my front pocket and pick loose a string with my finger. "How are you?" Each word comes out like a calculated step.

Ian doesn't immediately respond. "I'm doing all right." The silence hangs heavily.

Wow, that was such a smooth thing to say, Nora. He didn't just lose his daughter a couple months ago or anything.

"What can I help you with?"

I clear my throat. "Well, I was hoping you might know of some land. I mean land for lease. Wade is getting off this place, but he would like to find a new place to take the heifers if he can."

He probably doesn't know Wade, but too late now.

"A lot of land is changing hands right now. The drought's cracked down on everyone." Papers ruffle. "I tell you what, why don't you meet me in town for lunch, and we can talk over the details?"

Lunch? I've already had lunch. Well, at least I tried to eat. "You, you should talk to Wade. I don't really know what he's looking for, just that we need a place to go with these girls."

"Does Wade drive those crazy heifers all over the country looking for one little 'ole calf?"

My left index finger has just enough nail hanging that I can chew on it. "Well, no."

He chuckles. "I didn't think so. I'll meet you in town tomorrow at one, if that works for you."

Tomorrow, tomorrow, tomorrow. What day of the week is tomorrow? Oh, well, it's not like I have a social life that it would conflict with. "Yes, sir, I can do that."

"Sounds good. Talk to you tomorrow. M'bye."

I blink a few times. The phone clicks. "Bye." I mumble the word under my breath as the phone beeps its parting sound. I melt into the chair and rest my elbows on my knees.

You did it, Nora. You got the help. Now you just have to string words together in a coherent way.

***

Night checks aren't hard to make, because I can't sleep anyway. Over a dozen pieces of paper are wadded up in the trash can, the remains of my attempts to make a list of questions to ask. They all sound stupid. I don't know what to look for in land.

I mean, grass would be a nice start. Good fences and a sturdy set of pens, a bonus. If we're getting luxurious, a barn with lights and a smooth running chute. Okay, so maybe it's not so hard, but what if Wade wants other things? What's his budget, anyway? And how big of a place does he want?

Talks about downsizing have been a dime a dozen, even from Wade. He may have more money than I can shake a stick at, but he does have sense. Sense enough to cut his losses when he needs to.

I empty the glass of water I left on the counter that morning in one gulp. I've just grabbed the block of cheese from the nearly empty fridge when my phone quacks from the table.

Voicemail from Dad. Two minutes ago.

My finger hovers over the notification a moment before tapping it, and I lift the device to my ear.

"Hey Nora, I talked to Dave today. He's always got a receptionist job at his crop insurance company when you get things cleared off down there. Catch you later. Bye."

When. No *if*.

No *if you want*.

No *I love you*.

Not even *how are you doing?*

I sigh and set the phone down, staring at it. My shoulders slump, and I retrace my steps to the door. The idea of eating cheese puts a sour taste in my mouth. Any glow the morning still held vanishes, taken away by a ten-second voicemail.

Why did I think it would be different? He didn't like it when I jumped into ranching right out of high school.

A light breeze plays with the leaves of the big mesquite tree out the door. I rest my hand against the glass, and ever so slightly, I finger imaginary leaves.

Who said I need a place to go, anyway? Clearing off and selling out are two different things. Clearing off is inevitable, and needed. Selling out is not. There are ways to prevent it. I set my jaw and stalk to my bedroom. Speaking of doing something to prevent selling out, I have lunch to get to.

I have to dig past a dozen plaid and holey shirts before getting to the dark jeans and pastel pink shirt I'm looking for. A new layer of deodorant ought to mask the sweat I have shed. The jean legs slide snuggly over my dark blue stove top boots, also courtesy of the back of my closet.

In the bathroom, I take note of the hairs frizzing out from my braid and the inch-wide band creased around the top of my head. Great. The crease won't be a big deal, but even for me it's a bit too ratty of a braid to be going to town. To rebraid or do something a little nicer?

I glance through the doorway to a clock on the wall. Yikes! Wavy, semi-ratted hair it is. Running a brush through it is about as painful as running a shaggy poodle through a patch of catclaw, but I do it anyway.

Out the door and to my pickup, my heart is already racing. Down the road my left knee bounces wildly, speeding up with each passing mile. There is only one place in town to eat that's good anyway. I stop at the one blinking light and turn into the parking lot. 12:45. As usual, plenty of time to contemplate how awkward this is going to be!

For the next ten minutes, I organize the receipts in the console, three times. *Lord, I can't avoid this any longer, and avoiding it won't make it any less awkward. I'd like to ask you to help me not be so awkward, but I'm not even sure that's something I'm supposed to pray for.* I sigh. *Just bring about what you see fit from this meeting, God.*

A deep breath does nothing for the lead knot in the pit of my stomach. The pickup door feels heavier than it ought to. Half-expecting my legs to fail me, I hold onto the pickup door for a long moment.

It's Ian. My uncle. I sigh. The one that is the epitome of a good hand that has his life together. Not to mention the one that I've decided to make my saving grace from that blasted crop insurance desk. No pressure. At all.

Greasy air enters my nose even before I get to the front door. Inside, the chatter of a full room bombards me. I was hoping it would be a lot quieter. I step to the left to let the person behind me in and bump right into a broad build of a man. "I'm sorry," I mumble halfway under my breath as I tilt my head up.

Ian. *Think of things to say!*

Our eyes meet for a split second before my gaze shoots to a Charles Russel painting on the wall.

A low chuckle vibrates out of his chest. "Well, hello! It's not usually this crowded by now." He sweeps his hat off in one hand, and the other envelopes me in an awkward hug. "How are you?"

Without thought, I reach to adjust my hat back into place. "Good." I nod. *I think.* "You?"

"Staying busy," he says, just as a waitress motions us to follow her.

Thank you, Lord, that they give us menus right away. I already know what I want, but I don't know what to do with my hands.

"So, Wade's looking to move on."

At the sound of his voice, I jerk the menu away from my face and wince as it slaps the table. *Great start, Nora.*

I nod in reply. What am I supposed to say? Is it pushy to ask if he thinks he can help? Maybe he doesn't even want to. But then why would he have asked me to meet him here?

My eyes dart from the tables around us to the pictures on the wall and then spare a New York second to look at Ian. He's looking at me. My breath catches in my chest. Did I wash my face before I left? I definitely didn't put mascara on, so I can't have raccoon eyes.

"Sorry," he says quietly. "I forgot you and Kayla had the same eyes."

I grip the menu until my knuckles turn white. I never knew Kayla well, but from the few family get-togethers we did have, I know Kayla and Ian had a tight daddy-daughter relationship.

The waitress comes for our orders, giving me a good reason not to reply to that, but she also takes our menus, leaving me without a thing to do with my hands. I fish for my jacket pockets, but they aren't there, because it's eighty-five degrees outside and I left it at home.

Well, this lunch should be good and awkward.

Chapter 4

"Sure, I'd love to."

The words had come tumbling out of my mouth before the meaning could slap me upside the head. I agreed to go to Ian's house for supper next Sunday. His *house.* As the guest, am I supposed to take food, or is that infringing upon hospitality? No, that's what normal people do, right? So what do I take?

At least I have a few days to figure that out.

The tractor jerks, jarring my attention back to the present moment. The rickety old thing lurches into the row of haygrazer round bales. I ease the level forward, and it jerks the bale into the air. Gee, this thing is a safety hazard.

All the questions Ian asked me got answered about as well as this thing operates.

I lower the bale onto the flatbed of the ranch pickup and leave the tractor to idle.

Lease or no lease, I have to say goodbye to this place. Even if it rained an inch a week for the next couple months, it wouldn't bring this place back without a good rest.

I smash the brake to keep from plowing over the heifers.

I don't have to wish them goodbye, though. Not yet, and not if I can help it.

In the middle of a new greasewood patch, a couple hundred yards off the road, I gas it in reverse. Then I grate on the brakes and watch the hay bale roll off the back of the pickup. It flops over and is instantly mobbed by the heifers. Their horns clatter against one another as they push and shove in and out of the madness.

"Hey, girls!" I wave my arms from outside the circle. "Hey, let me through, and then you can have the whole thing." They part, making a little path a couple feet wide. Keeping one eye over my shoulder, I cut the twine off. Getting stabbed or run over is not on today's to-do list. The green wrapping frees tiny hay particles that get swept up in a whirlwind. Anywhere that wasn't dirty is now.

In the rearview mirror, I watch as they scrub their horns against the bale. Chunks of hay fly through the air and land against the next bush. A heifer throws her tail in the air and does a running buck around to the other side of the bale. I chuckle. It's the little things that make their day. And mine too, I guess, because this is it. This is why I have to go to that supper.

***

I finger the ends of my freshly washed hair. The time has arrived. With a bag of corn chips and a jar of salsa in one arm, I use the other to slam the pickup door behind me.

Deep breaths. Hopefully these steps look more sure than I feel. The one night I wouldn't have minded two heifers calving and one of them not take her calf, all's quiet in the pens.

I have to do this. I can do this. I will do this.

Maybe if I chant it to myself enough it will be true. I reach up to knock on the sparkling glass door, but before I can, the wooden one beyond it swings back. Ian's wife, uh, what is her name? Debra? No, Donnie? I haven't seen her too many times in my life, but man, I should know it. Denise? Yes. Denise smiles and waves me in.

As soon as I'm in the doorway, she wraps me in an unorganized hug. "So glad you could make it, sweetie!"

"Thank you for having me." I hold up the chips and salsa. "I brought chips."

Her face beams with a little too bright of a smile. "Oh, good! They will go great with enchiladas."

At least they're both Mexican foods.

Ian comes around the corner, padded mittens on his hands. They look foreign on him. He pulls them off and gives me a hug that manages to be a little less awkward than the one at the cafe.

"Thank you for coming." His voice is a tick quieter than the level of rustling Denise makes in the kitchen.

I smile and drop the arm I gave him a stiff-ish hug with.

Ian leads the way to the table. Pictures line the wall in a couple collections. Pictures with horses, mainly, a few family-style ones sprinkled in.

Denise deposits a bowl of salad on one end of the table and the bowl of chips on the other end. "All right, let's eat!"

There are four chairs. Denise has her hand on the back of one, so that's one down. Where does Ian usually sit? Which one am I supposed to sit at?

"Have a seat," Denise prompts.

I feel sweat push at the pores in the palms of my hands. Slapping on a smile, I hope I don't look as panicked as I feel. *Sit in the chair closest to the wall; it's always a safe option.* Ian sits in the chair to my left, and I try to breathe a little freer, but it doesn't work.

Ian and Denise bow their heads, and I quickly duck mine. It's been a long time since I've done this. Softly, Ian offers a short prayer, much like the ones my dad did growing up. Maybe that's how my grandpa did it when they were growing up.

A spatula in one hand, dishing out enchiladas, Denise asks, "So, Nora, Ian tells me you really enjoy your job. What's your favorite part?"

Without moving my head, I glance at Ian, who is absorbed in spreading his food out. "Uh, yes ma'am, I do." Gee, this is going to sound weird. "I guess that each calf on the ground is like an everyday miracle."

That blinding bright smile is on Denise's lips again. Has it left once this whole time? "They're so adorable."

I stuff a forkful of food in my mouth. Mmm, it's been a long time since I've had enchiladas like this. Smooth and flavorful, but no instant heartburn attached.

"How's your big project colt doing?"

I stop midchew. Of all the things we talked about at lunch the other day, Cante was not one of them. Even though it was a small bite, I have to swallow a couple times to get that bite down. How does he know about my project pony? Both of them are looking at me, and I realize how long I've been stalling. Paste on the smile again. One more swallow. "Cante is getting there." Ian nods in recognition of the name. "He's slow in coming out of his scaredy-catness."

"Do you need another one? I've got a four-year-old palomino that needs some using."

A thick silence instantly fills the air, and Denise shoots him a pointed look.

No idea what that was about. I shrug. "Sure, what's one more? It's not much fun if you don't keep at least one of those kind around. I enjoy it."

Through the rest of the meal, the only unprompted things I manage to get my brain to say are a couple comments on how good the food is. I can't get over the fact that Ian knew about Cante. I didn't even have Cante at the last family Christmas.

After chocolate sheet cake, to the living room we go. I sink into a leather chair that envelops me like a hug. I could take a nap in this one.

Ian grabs a handful of papers and sits in the chair next to me. "These are five or six leases I found. Not all of them are real close, but they are options." He stops thumbing through them to slide a picture of green grass tilted in a wave towards me. "Some even get rain every once in a while."

I crack a grin. "Wouldn't that be nice?"

"Tell me about it." He nods to the papers as I rotate one to the back of the stack. "Some of them are listed, but several are friends of mine. If you want to go check them out, let me know."

I look up at him, the corner of my lips curving up. He does know I'm not the one that needs to be looking at these, right? I just want a piece of land. As much as it pains me every time I unwrap that green net, I'll do it all year if I get to keep walking these girls into momma cows. Shame on me for thinking so, but I can't help it.

Denise comes and settles in the chair beside Ian. "Ian has been hammered with buyers. Big city folks think that this is a good time to buy, but they don't know the rancher."

His lips press into a thin line, and he stares out the window. "They don't give it up easy." He catches my gaze. "I hate it when they do sell, even if it is good for business. The young ones that want in the business can't afford it, so it goes to some bigwig that wants a toy." An edge has climbed into his voice.

I nod. "Sad."

Denise puts a hand on his arm and smiles at me.

"A couple weeks back, I sold a place your dad and I grew up helping out." He shakes his head, and his gaze grows intense.

"One day we were gathering a pasture with a bunch of cedar breaks in it. I was on the outside and ran into a crippled bull. If I plodded him along, those guys would have given me up for lost and gone on without me. I wasn't much more than a kid."

I giggle quietly. 'Much more than a kid' can mean a big age bracket depending on who is telling the story.

"Your dad was next to me, so I loped over and found him. I told him I'd ride his spot too if he'd trail the bull in. I told him to be sure and take it slow." His mouth quirks a smile. "He was all excited until I kept badgering him to take it slow with that bull. Never did have time for that type of thing."

That last sentence is like a rock slung to my heart. That ain't no lie. Never had time to slow down and teach his kids much either.

Ian continues. "So he trotted over with me and I helped him get started before riding on. I had half the cow count in front of me when we got to the meeting spot. Nobody had seen Mike with the bull, but we gathered up and cut to the pens. We had the herd to the pens, sorted, and still no Mike.

"The boss sent me back to find him, since I was the one that left him. I left the pens in a long lope and went and went. I trotted a while, occasionally hollering for him. By the time I made it back to where I left him, I was thinking I might not ought to go home. Mom might nail my hide to the wall, especially when she found out I should have taken that bull in.

"Then finally I saw his odd-shaped hat bopping along. When I caught up to him, he didn't have a bull within a hundred yards, and I was back to wanting to wring his neck. He'd dogged that bull until he got on the prod, and hobbled around in circles after he'd fallen down and wouldn't get up." He shakes his head. "By the time we got him up and to the pens, they'd finished branding and sent two pickups to look for us. I didn't speak to him all the way home, I was so mad at him."

I lean back against the chair, an easy smile resting on my lips. This isn't a story I've heard from Dad. Not that it would be, since his older brother, or growing up at all, aren't things he has ever talked about much. What would it have been like to make memories like that with Macy and Miles when we were kids?

Ian launches into another story, and I'm transported to another time. A craving stirs up in my belly like a heifer drawn to green grass. A craving to hold onto this life and make memories like these.

Dusk settles heavily around the house, and I linger in the chair a couple minutes past the end of the story. It's time to set the alarm clock and make the first night check. Hopefully, two of those gals are going to calve tonight. I stand and retrieve my hat from by the door. "Night check is calling."

Ian stands with a knowing smile. "Let me know what Wade thinks about these." He hands me the papers and reaches to give me a hug, which I return. "Thank you for coming."

"Thank you for having me."

I give Denise a hug as well before stepping out the door and breathing in the sweet scent of being alone.

All forty miles home I rack my brain for the conversation I don't remember having that would have clued Ian in on Cante.

Chapter 5

Cante sidles up to the gate with a slight touch of my spur. Impressive what he can do when his head is in the game. I fiddle the latch loose, and he stands quietly.

"Heck of a morning." I wipe the cuff of my shirt across my face before pulling my saddle from his back. "You're getting better about paying attention to what's going on," I tell him as I slip the hackamore from his head.

I bet we trailed that crazy heifer five miles before she finally acknowledged that she has a calf. I shake my head. She was tight bagged and her brains had already gone out the window. By the twelfth time she turned back, Cante turned back with her before I got my spur in his shoulder. Good for him.

I watch the gelding roll in the soft dirt before turning to the barn. My gaze sweeps over the heifers in the pens. One 'ole gal looks like she just might spit a calf out anywhere within the next twenty-four to one hundred and sixty-eight hours.

The rocks crunch under my boots. That heifer wasn't pushing, was she? I turn on my heels and lean against the fence for a better look. She gets up, walks in a circle, and lies back down.

She probably hasn't been in labor too long. The first calf can take a while.

I hang the hackamore in the barn and flop my shotgun leggins off. I've been accused more than once of jumping in to help a heifer out a little too early. This time I'm going to give it a bit of time. Again I study all the signs. Even if she is only in the early stages, I don't like how things are adding up.

The water from the hose starts out warm but after a few seconds cools off, and I slurp a long drink. Much better; at least I can swallow something besides dirt.

Inside the heifer lot, I ease down the fence towards the loner. About the time I am close enough to get a good look at her back end, she turns. I crane my neck, and she starts pacing the fence. Helpful.

"Just give me a second to look, and I'll leave you alone."

I get in a good place for a look, and then she trots over to another fence and starts pacing it. I sigh and lean up against the fence. Clattering gates around and moving the other heifers really isn't going to help calm her down.

"Not much I can do about that, sister. I want to check out what you got going on." I open the gate into the alley and step around the other heifers, rousing them from their cud-chewing party. I stuff them in a pen and set the gates for Momma-to-be to go in the chute. It's a straight shot, theoretically simple.

She walks up into the snake alley. Her back hooves clatter against the sheet metal halfway up the pipe sides.

Already POed.

I can't say I blame her, though. I would be too if someone came in here harassing me while I was trying to have a baby.

As she takes hesitant steps up the snake, I watch her contract and release. She's having a baby. Now. And I like what I see even less than I thought I did. If this is as bad as it looks, I'm up a creek with no paddle. *Deep breath. We don't know what it actually is yet.*

"Come on, sis, get in that chute." Her two front feet step on the wood floor of the catch chute. "That a'girl." She runs back a few steps into a pipe I slid behind her. "The faster you get in here, the faster I can help you." I grit my teeth. "And hopefully save your baby. I've already lost too many to lose y'all too."

I snag a sorting stick from its spot leaning against the fence. Holding the gate into the catch chute with my left hand, I whack her with the sorting stick with my right. She leans back against the pipe harder.

"And this is why they use 'heifer' as an insult." My shoulders slump. This is definitely *not* helpful for the calf's chances of survival.

My arm burns from the strain of holding the gate.

One step, another. *That's it. Two more steps and this gate can slide in behind you.* She sniffs the pipes in front of her and takes another step forward. Score! The gate slams down. I cock the head gate in a hair and wait. As soon as her ears slide out, I push the lever back.

Now for the real work.

I roll up my shirt sleeves while trotting to the barn for thin plastic gloves that reach up to my shoulders. Darn that neighbor bull making these heifers throw big calves!

Back with the gloves, I slide the pipe in behind her and tie up the gate. Here goes nothing. I plop bits of lubricant goo on my blue plastic-covered arm. Just as I'm about to slide my hand in and check out the calf's position, the heifer bends in the middle and strains. There is no movement of the calf's position.

Once the heifer is relaxed, I slide my fingers over the bulge of slimy black fur. Nose, feet, even one foot would be good—something to work with. But a bulge? My heart rate picks up. I can't deliver a breech.

There is little space, but I push my hand deeper and deeper until I feel a hip and down the back leg. The cool drink I got turns in my stomach like a tidal wave. This is about as great as landing in a prickly pear. The heifer has a low chance that she'll make it out of this alive, or able to breed again, and that calf has an even lower chance of surviving.

I lean against the pipe fence and try to steady my heart. If it's running away, it's hard for my thoughts to stay together. The blue plastic sticks together as I strip it off my arm, turning it inside out. I lift my hat and let the breeze hit my forehead on the way to the house.

This time I have no problem picking up the phone and finding the contact I need.

"You've reached the mailbox of—" James' voice comes on to recite his name.

I tap my fingers on the table while I wait for it to beep, and then I start my message. "Hey James, are you in the area? I've got a breech calf I could use some help with. Give me a call back."

A heavy sigh does little to relieve the weight in my chest. I don't have time to wait on James to call me back. The nearest vet is an hour away; no way either the heifer or the calf would make it through the stress of that haul. Of course, this is the time that Wade decides to be on one of his trips, so he's no help.

In my hand my phone dings.

Just found out a few of the places have moved to for sale instead of lease.

Ian. Of course!

I try James again, but it hits the voicemail again. I don't leave a voicemail, but it sends my heart into a runaway as I find Ian's contact and hit call. Adrenaline and anxiety mix together like baking soda and vinegar.

"Hello?"

I jump half an inch worth. "Hi." I swallow the lump in my throat. "Um, do you know anything about breech calves?"

Wow, that was really smooth.

"Uh, yeah, I've dealt with a few of them. Can't say I've had much success though."

Better than no success. "You wouldn't be able to help me pull one, would you? One of the heifers has a big black calf that's breech." I bite my bottom lip, hard.

Papers shuffle. "Yeah, I'll be there in twenty minutes or so."

After the shallow breaths I've been taking, my lungs drink in the oxygen as I breathe easier. "Thank you. I can't get a'hold of James, and Wade is out of town." I give him directions before sliding my phone into my back pocket and barreling out the door.

While waiting on Ian, the minutes tick by slower than cold molasses drips out of a bottle. I pull the chains, calf puller, a whole box of gloves, lubricant, a cow halter, and a half-worn-out rope out of the barn and pile them up by the chute.

Every few minutes the heifer pushes on the chute, and the rusty junctions squeal. I release her head so that she can be a tiny bit more comfortable, not that I expect her to be any sort of comfortable with that big 'ole calf sitting the way it is.

I hear the purr of Ian's diesel and poke my head over the fence. A little smile of relief pops up on my face. "Afternoon!"

"Afternoon." He slips through the gate. "Let's see what we've got here." He takes the glove I have waiting for him. Once it's on his arm and lathered with lubricant gel, he slips his hand in to assess the situation. Shaking his head, he mutters, "She's sure got herself a fix, doesn't she?"

I nod, anxiously looking over his shoulder.

"We'll have to push his butt back in as much as we can so we can get ahold of the legs." Ian draws his hand out and adjusts the top of his glove.

My fingers drum on my leg at my side. I want to do something to help. Standing here watching over his shoulder reminds me of all the times I watched over my dad's shoulder as a little girl. I never got to do it myself with him, not even take a turn with the post-hole diggers. He didn't have time to wait on me to be awkward at it.

"Gets tight in there." Ian wiggles his fingers.

"Do you want me to take a turn?"

He looks over his shoulder at me, and a small smile turns up his lips. "Go for it! You can start fishing for those back legs."

I share his smile, but I'd venture to say mine is wider. As I slide my arm in as deep as I can, that smile fades to a thin line, and my eyebrows pinch together. There is a little bit more room than before, but it doesn't make it much easier to find those back legs. My fingers brush what feels like a hock, and I rotate my arm in an unnatural position to get a better grip on the leg. As I start to pull out, the heifer's cervical muscles grip my arm, putting that on hold.

"Getting anywhere?" Ian asks, leaning against the frame of the chute.

The heifer relaxes a bit, and my breathing becomes easier, as if she had a'hold of my chest, not my arm. "A little at a time. I've got a'hold of a hock." It would be real helpful to have both hands, but there sure as heck isn't room for that. The leg is bigger around than my hand can hold onto and keeps slipping out of my grasp about the time I think I've moved it.

Lord, let us get the little one out of here alive.

Pull, slip, readjust, another tug. After a few reps, I can tell for sure that I'm making progress. "It's coming," I whisper, squinting my eyes as I readjust my grasp. *Please. Don't. Slip now.* We've made too much progress to lose it now.

A yellowy-white hoof slides a couple inches out of the birth canal. Blood rushes down my arm and into my fingers, sweet, sweet blood flow.

Ian has a chain ready and slips it on the leg. "Nice work."

My smile comes back as I take the end of the chain and keep gentle pressure on it so that leg doesn't slip back in. As Ian starts the process of fetching the other leg, the heifer bellers.

I know, sis. Hang in there.

Time combats itself, feeling like we've been at this for hours, but then seeming like it has only been seconds. My arm burns with the tension of the chain, and a bead of sweat runs down the baby hairs at the sides of my face.

The rhythmic heavy breathing of the heifer is disrupted as she flails her feet against the sides of the chute. I want to assure her it will all be over soon, but that feels like more than a white lie.

The other leg is coming, though, right? I don't ask, just keep holding the chain.

Please let him get the other leg out, Lord.

A low groan fills the air as Ian rightens himself from a stooped position. I can't be sure if the noise came from him or the heifer, but by the look on Ian's face, it isn't a far-fetched idea to say it was him. I finger the loose end of the calving chain in my free hand, making a loop I drape over the hoof as soon as it emerges into open air.

Between two free hands and two hands holding legs, we get the chain in place on the leg. I take the loose bit of chain between the two feet in both my hands and recline against them in a steady pull. Slowly, I put my weight into it. Still nothing moves. An exhausted smile lifts my lips, and that age-old feeling of not having enough weight in my britches comes up again.

Ian chuckles behind me and takes hold of the chain closer to the heifer than my hands are. With the help, it feels like I'm pulling less, so I grit my teeth and pull harder. The calf doesn't move, even when the heifer lurches forward in the chute.

It slips, but what slipped? Did the calf really move, or is it just my hands? I readjust my sweaty hands on the chain. It happens again, and Ian says, "That's it. Come on, Momma, try."

A smile takes over my lips. It is working! I stand straighter just in time not to fall backward as the hips come free of the birth canal. Leaving the pulling up to Ian, I cradle the body in my arms as it finishes its immersion into the world. It slips fully into my cradle, heavy enough I nearly drop it.

I lay the calf in the midafternoon sun, afterbirth sticking to my shirt. Clawing at the sack around its nose, I clear its airway and then move to pumping its stomach. *Breathe, little one. Breathe.* A couple more pumps and then I rock back on my heels, studying for any sign of life. Nothing. I stick my hand in its mouth and clear mucus from it. *Come on. I've already lost too many. Not you, too.*

Ian squats beside me. "Breathing?"

I shake my head and stop my frantic revival efforts. The air leaves my lungs, deflating my chest. I slump into the dirt. Ian's hand squeezes my shoulder, and I look up at him.

"He didn't have a very good chance."

I nod. I know that, but it doesn't pick me up any. "How bad do you think she's tore up?" I look over my shoulder at the heifer.

"I wouldn't put money down that she'll breed up again, but I figure she'll survive."

One lingering look over the calf, and then I walk over to the chute. I strip the gloves from my arms. My boots feel heavy as I slug to the barn to rifle through the medicine cabinet. I find a big pink bolus and pull a dose of vitamins up in a syringe.

Ian takes the balling gun with the bolus in it and puts it down the heifer's throat while I give her the shot in the skin of her neck. He opens the head gate and she trots out.

The heifer walks up to the calf's body and sniffs it before she goes to the fence and starts pacing. My heart shatters in my chest, and my eyes sting. The what-ifs and maybes swirl full force. Maybe if I had just checked a little sooner. What if I could have pulled the calf by myself and gotten it done sooner? I squat down and start gathering all the used gloves off the ground. Really, there isn't anything I could have done differently. It's just a calf; they come and go anyway. It doesn't make me feel like any less of a failure, though.

I get things cleaned up and myself pulled together before joining Ian, leaning against the fence. The silence feels heavy, and a thousand questions push to come out. Finally, I spare a glance at Ian. I lick my lips. "How do you keep strength on these cattle right now?"

I feel his gaze swivel to me. He shakes his head. "It's hard to keep strength on anything right now." He sighs. "Pour the salt, mineral, and protein to them and give them all the roughage they want is about all we can do."

I press my lips together in a thin line. Not what I wanted to hear, but at least I'm doing the right things.

He nods towards the heifer. "These Herefords are hardy. They can make it on mesquite beans and prickly pear if they have to."

One side of my lips lifts in a sad smile. "Poor things won't know what to do if they ever do see a blade of grass."

Ian's sad chuckle expressed the resignation in my chest.

I can't help them have the strength to calve and raise their babies if I'm pushing papers in some office. I have to figure something out.

Chapter 6

"These are new options I found. Wade hasn't said anything about the ones from before?" Ian sets a briefcase on the corner of his desk and flips through it.

An exhausted laugh leaves my lungs. "No, last he told me he was going out of town and would have answers when he got back." I fan the papers he hands me.

"Sounds about right." He chuckles and tucks his folder back into the briefcase. "I talked to your dad the other day."

One of my eyebrows perks up. "Oh yeah?" *Since when do they talk to each other?*

Silence hangs in the air for several seconds. Finally, he glances at me and then back at his desk. "Yeah, he said he's got an insurance job for you, if you need it."

A moment passes as I chew on my bottom lip. "Is that what he said?" A voicemail telling me about it was apparently not enough.

Ian cocks his head.

I swallow my annoyance and paste on a smile. "I'm sure Wade will want to at least talk about something out of this pile." The papers rustle as I rotate my wrist.

Ian chuckles under his breath and shakes his head. "What's this about with your dad?" He perches a hip on the corner of the desk.

"Apparently, crop insurance is a good fit for me." I shrug, not looking at him. "They never got it. I don't know why I expect them to now."

"Never got what?" he prods.

So we are going to air this out, are we? I wince. This is not the prettiest part of my family's existence, though probably not the worst either. "Me. What I want out of life, the things I enjoy, why I do it."

I risk a glance into his eyes to find patience resting in them. He doesn't look like he's about to jump in and say something. A deep breath ignites my words. "Since I was a little girl, birth, specifically calving, has fascinated me. They didn't think taking this job straight out of high school was a good idea. It wasn't very secure." My voice mocks the last sentence.

Ian's gaze is intense for a long moment. "You don't look like a crop insurance salesman."

A smile pushes past my pursed lips. I feel light and almost laugh, but Ian's face turns thoughtful.

"Being secure isn't all there is to life. A reining horse gets so good at turning around that it never gets to really show that off and spin around to stop a cow."

I fling my hand out to my side. "See! That's what I keep thinking. Dad's getting his 401K built up, but he's miserable while he's doing it." I take a breath and tuck my hand back in my pocket where it belongs.

Ian nods. "It happens to the best of us."

The blood in my veins freezes. Is Ian really miserable doing real estate?

***

On the drive home from Ian's office, I replay his words. He agreed with me. More than that, he gets it. He gets me, what makes me tick. A smile like the gentle yellow of a prickly pear bloom spreads across my face.

With a sudden burst of courage, I take the turn to Wade's house instead of my own. He just got back from his jaunt, so maybe he'll be in a land-discussing frame of mind.

The out-of-place oak tree shades my pickup as I pull up beside the gray Dodge. A terrier comes yapping from the porch.

Wade's voice bellers from the house before he does. "Scrappy, shut up!"

I step from the cab and reach down to pet the little dog. "Hi, Scrappy." I pick him up and start for the porch.

"Well, good afternoon!" Wade stands half in, half out of the screen door, his Hawaiian shirt rippling in the wind.

I smile and scratch behind the dog's ear.

"Come on in here." He tilts his head and wags his finger at Scrappy as I tote him by Wade. "Scrappy, you found someone to mooch off of."

The door slams, jerked by the spring at the top, and I lean my hat up against the wall behind a red chair. A breeze blows through the house, briefly pushing out the musty smell.

"What brings you by?"

I produce the papers from behind Scrappy. "I saw Ian in town today, and he had some more options for you." I hand them over and scratch the terrier again before asking, "Have you seen anything you're interested in?"

He studies the papers, giving each a scrutinizing glare. "These look like nice places for someone's sister's brother-in-law's cousin, but they aren't for what I need." He rifles through the pages and sticks one out to me. "Two hundred acres two hours away isn't worth the fuel it'd take to get them there, even if it does rain every other week."

I stick my free hand in my pocket and nod. There are no grounds for argument, but Ian is doing the best he can. Two hundred acres around Abilene wasn't going to hold any more than the twenty sections we had here. They get more rain than our three times a year, but not *that* much more. Do we look six hours away, where it really rains every week?

Wade shakes his head. "It's going to have to have room for some yearlings too if it is going to be that far away. Shipping is too expensive."

Scrappy wiggles in my arms, and I release him to the ground. There goes my toy to hide my hands behind. And so much for Wade being in a land-discussing state of mind. "Well, I better get back out to the house."

He looks up. "Where are we at on the calf count?"

Right. Calf counts, updates, communication. Those are still things.

I spout off some numbers. "They've been busy this past week. Thankfully, only one has had a hard time with it."

She had a hard enough time for all of them, though.

"How many blackies are we getting?"

I count on my fingers, running pictures of the pairs through my mind. "Only four on the ground."

He turns behind him and grabs a quart jar of tea. "Maybe we'll make out better than I thought."

The dog scratches on the door. I pick up my hat.

"I'll get by to look at the new calves this week."

"They'll be out with the rest of them," I say, trying to put air in my voice. Donning my hat, I push the screen door open.

The engine of my pickup rattles to life, churning the disappointment and defeat together in my stomach.

Now what? Does Wade even want to find a lease? Ian has looked in every nook and cranny. How much more can I ask of him?

***

The next morning, wind swirls dust from the pens through the gaps around the house windows. Through the haze I gaze over the heavies. They lie around, chilling, chewing their cuds. I sneeze and turn to the house. Sinking into my fluffy brown chair in the den, I take the end of my braid and weave it through my fingers.

That crop insurance desk keeps getting closer. I grip the chair. But dang it! I am trying. Trying everything I know to keep from ending up in it.

On the round table beside me, my phone lights up with a text. I glance over at it. No one talks to me, especially texts. Curiosity gets the best of me, and I reach for the phone. Its coolness slides into my hand.

Attachment: 1

I thought you might enjoy this.

I don't give them permission, but sunflower smiles sprout on my face. The half grin I've seen on Ian's face pops into my mind's eye. The picture has two red-and-white calves perched on top of a curly-headed bull with little stubbed horns. A childish giggle jiggles my chest. One calf has three feet on the bull, the spare one balancing halfway between the earth and the bull's back.

They look like they're enjoying themselves.

I add a simple smiley face but delete it before hitting send. When my phone has just touched the thin denim above my knee, it lights back up.

Yes they are.

So Wade—Erase. *Wade*—Erase. *I guess that insurance job really does have my name on it.*

The cursor blinks at me, and I read the message I typed out, twice. It sounds like I am complaining, and Ian doesn't have time to listen to me complain. The phone starts vibrating, and Ian's name is at the top of the screen. My heart rate spikes. I take a couple deep breaths and pick it back up. "Hello."

"Afternoon." There is a pause. "I forgot to tell you I'm going to be out of the office for the rest of the week, but give me a call if you need anything."

I nod then quickly reply, "Sounds good." Questions pulse through my mind, alternating with things I want to tell him.

"What do you have going on this afternoon?"

He's still on the phone! I take a deep breath. "Uh, well, I'm holding this chair down right now." The chuckle that comes across the phone line puts a smile on my face. It's low and gentle. A sigh sits heavily in my lungs, though. I wrap my hair around my index finger again.

Ian doesn't have time to listen to my problems.

"That sounds like a pretty good deal."

I wet my lips. The words mill on my tongue, looking for any opportunity to shoot out. The silence spans a moment longer, and the words find one to take. "So I dropped by Wade's."

"Oh yeah? What did he have to say?"

"He's not a fan." The sigh escapes and so do a whole thicket of words. "I get that he has to look on the money side of things, but is he even trying to like a place?" I lean my head against the back of the chair. "I can't save them all, but dang it, it's better than not trying. For every calf that doesn't make it, there's three that do. I don't claim to be the best. I just say I try. So now what? I give up and push papers? I can't sign the lease for him."

A few seconds pass.

Holy moly, I just spilled a whole bunch of murky water all over Ian.

My breath comes in short spurts before I stop to make sure he's even still on the phone.

That's when he says, "You don't have to push papers, even if he doesn't sign a lease. There are lots of other cows, even heifers in the world. And you still have time."

Time. I look at the calendar over the round table. Not too much of it remains. Six weeks are all we have left until the move-off date. Again I nod my head before remembering he can't see it, but I don't know what to say. I clear my throat. "I hope so."

We slip into a little small talk before hanging up.

I slide my phone onto the table beside the chair and stare at the ceiling. Maybe there's more options besides pushing papers than what I thought. I reach for the couple-week-old *Livestock Weekly* that Sam gave me that sits on the side table, and I scan the classifieds on the last couple pages. Most of the jobs are farther east into Texas.

Folding the paper up, I shrug off the idea of a new job. What did Ian say? We still have time.

***

Dune comes trotting up with Banks, stumbling before dropping to a walk. I toss the bit of cake I saved back from the heifers for them. I lean against the fence, watching the two eat. What happens to the three steeds if I start pushing papers? They don't like aimless trail rides any more than I do. Not to mention what Cante would become standing up in a pen eating good feed without work. I switch my eyes to the three-year-old behind me. A nightmare, souped up enough to try something that proves him as tough as his name.

Taco soup minus the soupy part that I pull out of the fridge grows cold again in my bowl. My fork shuffles the meat back and forth from one side to the other. Eating sounds about as grand as if it were buzzard soup. My enthusiasm for life in general doesn't get much better after a hot shower and sliding into bed. I flip, flop, toss, and turn.

I haven't slept a wink when I get up for the first night check. A body ambles from behind the hay bale, and I perk up. Maybe a baby will be on the way, and there will be a purpose for why I'm not sleeping. But it's just the heifer we pulled the calf from, who sticks her head in the hay bale and sets to eating. So much for having a reason to stay up.

Spending more dark hours awake than asleep is awful, and even worse when I don't have a good reason. I do have a reason and arguably a good one, but it falls into the second category of the quote "Change what you can and give what you can't to God."

Between night checks, I pray another patched-together prayer, clutching my pillow.

God, I can't do anything about it, but you can. I know you have a plan. And you know I don't know what it is, and how hard of a time I'm having waiting on it. Please help me get some sleep tonight.

I turn over, staring into the darkness.

Knock me out for a while if you have to.

After I have looked in at the five heavies in the hue of the early morning, I put myself back to bed. I don't even bother to take my boots off and get between the covers. There's not time enough for much more than a nap anyway.

The trill of my ringing phone wakes me. I blink several times before swallowing and saying, "Hello."

"Good morning." The teasing in Ian's voice makes me want to crawl under the bed.

My boot heels hit the floor, and I absently straighten the blanket on top of the bed. "Good morning."

"How about a road trip tomorrow?"

Tomorrow? I don't even know what day it is. "Uh, sure." The air gets cooler the closer to the kitchen I get. I squint against the glaring sun and down a cup of water.

"Good. I've got a lease we're going to look at. Wade is pretty excited about it."

Wade already knows. I set the cup down and push away the pang inside. But Wade actually found something he likes enough to look at! "Wow, that's impressive. Where's it at?"

His voice is light, like the birds outside the window. Is that a smile I hear? "Four hours northeast of here in Huntsburrow."

I push my lips up, even if he can't see them. "It must be pretty nice if he's going that far to check it out."

"I'm hoping it lives up to his list of qualifications." Scuffling sounds rise in the background. They clear a little for him to say, "We're meeting in town at the arena at eight in the morning. I've got to get going, but I wanted to let you know."

"Thanks for calling. See you tomorrow."

The phone beeps its ending tone, and I blow out a breath. I stop fighting the grin away. My lips just won't stay straight.

We're actually doing this.

Chapter 7

"With any luck we'll have us a future secured today," I tell the heifers, watching them push their way around the trough. *God, please let this work.* I push a breath through my lips. *But not my will.*

When I get back in the house, I throw the covers up on my bed and lay bacon in sizzling grease. Scrambled eggs with a couple pieces of that bacon on top, rolled up in a tortilla, makes for one of the fullest breakfasts I've made in a while.

The seafoam button-down and dark bootcut jeans I dig up from the back of the closet bear the signs of the months they've been back there. I drag out a dust-bunny-littered ironing board and an iron that looks like it belongs a generation back.

By the time daylight springs, my clothes are ready, but I don't chance putting them on yet. I make one more round by the heifers and move a few spare T-posts out of the back of my pickup. The last several weeks, I have put more miles on the old thing than I have in the last six months.

After piddling around so long, I finally slide into my freshly ironed yet not quite pressed clothes at seven fifteen. I walk out the door five minutes later and watch the world swirl by.

In the lot beside the arena, my knee bounces the minutes by, waiting on the two men to join me and kick off the adventure. According to the old cattlemen, daylight has sprung, though most of the rest of the world wouldn't quite call it that. The orange glow on the horizon stretches miles long, but only looks a couple inches tall. The fiery orange ball has yet to show itself for the day.

A couple cottontails nibble breakfast off the grass spotted around the lot. They timidly hop from one to the next, occasionally standing up on their hind legs to wiggle their noses.

One is in that position when suddenly it darts and is gone, its friend right behind it. I accept the loss of my entertainment with a sideways twitch of my lips. Then I hear it: the hum of a diesel. That must be what sent the rabbits scurrying. Before the diesel rounds the bend, bright white headlights bombard my mirrors from behind.

A pickup pulls up on either side of me almost in unison. I slide my wallet into my front jean pocket and my phone into the inside pocket of my denim jacket. Leaning across the seat, I slam my fist down on the manual lock. A puff of ten-year-old decaying foam sends me into a coughing fit. Maybe it will taint some of that sparkling cleanliness I left the house with.

Ian and Wade are already standing in front of my pickup talking. I put on a smile and take a deep breath. "Good morning, gentlemen."

"Morning," Wade bellows, smacking my shoulder and shaking my hand.

My smile holds real life then. I start to bring my right hand up again to shake Ian's hand, but at the same time my left arm starts to leave my side too. Ah, what am I doing? My heart lurches like a standard transmission that missed a gear.

Don't embarrass yourself this early in the morning. You've got to spend all day with them.

Ian saves me with a wide swoop of his arm. "How are you this morning, girl?"

My left arm finishes its hugging act, my right one coming around in a halfhearted, awkward sort. "Good, you?" The words bubble out, half halted by him squeezing my rib cage.

"Ready to go!"

Wade rubs his hands together. "Take off and I'll follow."

I freeze. My eyelids don't even blink. Who am I supposed to ride with? I push my hands into the joke of a back pocket in my jeans.

Ian stops at the off corner of his pickup bed. "You walking?"

I try to smile as I slide in the passenger's seat. The cab practically sparkles; it is so clean. My hands sit folded in my lap as I look around.

"You're allowed to sit in the seat, you know."

A little nervous laugh bubbles out as I adjust myself within the two raised edges of the passenger's seat. With each inhale, I take stock of the smell—subtle but assaulting all at once. Instead of being stuffy and dry, it is, well, the opposite. Clean. Fresh.

"I try to keep it looking new. Being a real estate agent, people kinda frown if you show up in a beat-up pickup."

I glance at him before fixing my gaze out the window once again. How does he do that? Maybe it was my eyes as I took in the pickup. "So what's this place like?"

"Twelve sections, pretty nice fences, a shiny new pen set up." His left wrist rests on the top of the steering wheel. "There's a couple of dirt tanks scattered around."

My eyebrows lift. Why are they leasing such a nice place out? Especially if those tanks have water in them.

"Kids of the couple that have it decided they didn't want to keep up with it anymore. They've all got city jobs."

I shake my head. "It's sad. Some of us would give our right arm to have a little piece of land to run livestock on, and those that have it coming to them can't see past the next technology gadget." One day it would be nice to have a spread of my own. Maybe with a husband, if that comes about.

Ian nods while I speak, before adding, "And everybody is going to get hungry one of these days and decide maybe raising your own meat isn't such a bad deal after all."

"Exactly."

The conversation lulls and I zone out, watching the green bar ditches go on for miles. In a week's worth of afternoons, I could put some flesh on those heifers if I had bar ditches like that at home.

Pop! Ian's hand smacks the console.

I jump, and my head swings toward him. I breathe faster, trying to recover.

Ian is laughing so hard, I wonder if he can see where he's going. It's infectious and I end up laughing too.

"You almost jumped out that window." His words are broken apart by bits of laughter.

I shake my head, but can't keep a straight face. This guy is impossible! It's been a long time since anyone has played that trick on me. A long time.

Ian turns left onto a red dirt road. Mesquites dot the pasture, but these aren't scrawny bushes. They are real trees complete with gnarly twists in branches the size of soccer balls. Green stuff half a foot tall stands in the bar ditches, but it doesn't stop there. Evidently barbed wire doesn't stop the growth of it in this end of the world. Into the pastures it grows, occasionally shortened by teeth.

The pickup comes to a stop at a gate over a cattle guard. The fences to each side are so new, the wire still gleams silver in the sunlight. With a grin, and raised eyebrows I take it in and then look over at Ian. He too grins.

"It's the gold lock on top." He holds out a key on a piece of leather string.

I take the key from him and lower myself into freshly cut grass. I fumble the lock around, sweat already forming on my forehead under my hat. The gate's high-pitched scream assaults my ears as I push it back.

A bead of sweat runs down my forehead and melts into my hat band. Ian's pickup bumps over the pipes and comes to a stop with the passenger door in line with me. Humidity. I haven't felt it in quite a while.

"You allergic to the wet?" That amused grin pulls at Ian's lips.

For a moment I just look at him, then I run my wrist over my top lip. Right. That. I crack a grin. "Maybe it's all this sitting." Hopefully that sounds as light as I meant it.

Bermuda grass with rich green leaves waves in the light breeze. It's tall enough it lies over on itself. It'd take my three ponies a month or more to put a heart on a trap like this. *I bet that's the kind of grass chiggers live in, though.*

Like a kid at the circus, I can't take it all in fast enough, even at ten miles an hour. Everything is so fresh and rich looking. We jostle down the road a couple miles before barn red starts showing up between the patchwork of leaves. The gates have horseback latches.

"Those pens have hardly seen cattle." Ian's eyes linger on the pens until the pickup hits a hole, shaking us up inside the cab. "I'd bring a load of nice gravel in on this road. When it comes a good rain, it gets slick." Ian eases the pickup to a stop, putting my window looking right down the loading chute.

The grate floor has angle iron steps going up it. It doesn't even look like there is a green cow stain on it. A shiny sight.

Ian's door opens, and he steps out to talk with Wade. The rattle of the gray's engine dies away, and I push the door open. I slide into the back seat, moving a sorting flag to the floorboard. Wade folds himself in the cab, and my stomach snaps to attention like a border collie caught lying down.

Lit up like a kid in a candy store, Wade looks back at me. "It's new and shiny."

"Sure is." My voice comes out quieter than it sounds in my head. I look again at the pens. Not even an annoying tree has tried to grow up in a gate. "Those heifers will think they've jumped off into heaven with all this grass."

New green grass pokes up all around the old dry grass left by the fall frost. I won't be putting hay out, just riding to check under every tree to keep counts. I smile.

No more dulling knives with baling twine.

"Wouldn't they? Those pairs James has could fill up out here too."

I press my lips into a thin line. *There might not be enough grass for* that.

On the way home, after listening to Wade talk Ian's ear off through a delicious lunch, my inner smile starts to fade. We only spent three or four hours between looking around and eating lunch, but it will nearly be dark when I roll back into that cozy little dust pit.

No lunch chats with Ian.

Whoa, where did that come from? What does it matter, anyway? Practically every time I talk to him, I'm on pins and needles.

"What cloud rained on your parade?"

I jump a little and look out the window to hide the flush on my cheeks. "What parade?"

"Well, I don't know what parade it was, but you were having a parade." Ian chuckles.

"How do you know?"

He shakes his head, studying me for as long of a moment as driving allows him. "Why don't you quit avoiding the question?"

"You're avoiding one too." I bite my bottom lip, but the smile still shows. When his eyes cut across the console at me, the smile drops. The silence that follows tugs at the truth string in my chest. "I was thinking it's quite the drive out here, is all."

Silence again. He is probably asking the same question I've been asking myself. Since when has it bothered me? "For Wade to keep an eye on the calves the way he likes to."

Ian nods, and his silence speaks louder than words could. It pulls on that truth string again.

Putting up with a little humidity is a small sacrifice to keep from pushing crop papers around an inky office. Somehow, telling myself that doesn't bring as much comfort as it should. A pang for something left behind pops against my heart.

"So how'd you find this place?" Questions. I am asking him a real question.

He repositioned his hands on the steering wheel to be able to rest both elbows. "Wellman and Kay have been like family to me since I left home. Their kids missed the gene, and I'd told them I wanted to have—I told them I'd help them find someone they could trust to lease it out to."

When he left home. Daddy never talks about growing up, let alone when Ian left home. When had he left? "That's nice." I play with an old medicine bottle tab in my jacket pocket. The jacket I didn't take off even though it warmed up considerably.

Ian has a little bunch of cows. Is it too far for him to drive to have them out there? Like the rest of us, he probably feeds them every drop they get. Rain, we all need rain down here.

A heavy sigh leaves my chest without permission.

Ian looks over with raised eyebrows.

Is there a shade darker than scarlet? If so, it is on my cheeks. That sigh was not supposed to be released around other humans. Maybe he will just forget it happened, but the slight smirk under his mustache clearly indicates that will not be happening.

"What's that about?"

Can the pickup floorboard just come loose and swallow me up? "Nothing at all." Under my hat brim, I steal another glance at the smirk.

A deep vibrating laugh fills the cab, and Ian's big hand rumples my shoulder. "Is that a girl sigh?"

Ah! I've become a dramatic girl. Like the ones that always talk about boys in the back of Sunday school. Bringing my arms up, I hide behind them. Too bad his seats are clean. If this were my pickup I would pull my heels up on the seat to hide behind too.

"Oh, come on. It wasn't that bad."

I unhide myself, cheeks still flushed. *The passing trees are very pretty. Oh, and look, it's a rock.*

Ian chuckles again.

"There's no chance that's going to be erased from your memory, is there?"

The smug happiness still hasn't left his face. "Very, very low chance." I have time to nod before he adds, "But I won't bring it up in public."

I smile with him. "I guess I can't ask for much more."

Chapter 8

Wade's taking his slow, sweet time.

"I'll let you know when I make a decision." Those were Wade's parting words to me from the arena *three* days ago.

I open the plate cabinet and pull a blue tin one down, wiping the dust out of it with the sleeve of my shirt. The breathability of the house. That is something I will not miss. Houses aren't supposed to be known for breathability.

My grilled cheese oozes beans and cream cheese as I plop it down on the plate. I shake my hand, willing the heat to fly off the end of my fingers. There are too many layers of calluses for it to leave a burn.

The heifers are fine, great, grand even, and still not calving. There is always one I can go hunt up from under a wanna-be tree, but there really is no need in it. Not when the move is looming in the air like a thundercloud that may or may not drop rain. I'll be busier than I want to be in a couple weeks, lease or not.

Halfway through my sandwich, I narrow my eyes at the counter beside the sink. One person doesn't use but one of each dish—okay, maybe two. I leave the sandwich to rifle around the spare bedroom until I find a medium-sized cardboard box. On my way by the table, I take a hunk out of the sandwich with my teeth. It's like the drive-by snacks of mesquite leaves Cante takes.

The tin plates fit nicely in the bottom of the box. Slide them in, one and done. Putting the coffee mugs around them isn't quite so easy. I turn one with the handle up and then out to the side. Not working. I cock my head. Two clang together, and my back muscles bristle.

I'd kinda like them to make the move, if possible. Leaving them on the counter, I track back to the spare room, grabbing a handful of tortilla chips on my way by the table. I tote the whole box full of old newspapers into the kitchen with me.

I have been avoiding the whole moving thing for a while, but I've not been so far into denial that I haven't prepared for it.

The spruced-up grilled cheese has grown cold long before I come back to it, three boxes of kitchen stuff packed later. The Huntsburrow place has room for twice as many dishes.

On a roll I tape the bottom of a few more boxes and stack towels and sheets in them. Three weeks isn't too long to live without the extras. As I plunge into my closet, I have a brief moment of doubt on that matter, but I discard it and keep going.

When I've hauled all my shirts from the closet, they look like a lot more than they ever have from the door of the closet. There's a half a box of shirts that I haven't worn in six months and a stack on my bed eighteen inches high. Crossed-legged in the middle of my floor, I'm surrounded by various piles of clothes. Fold these to give away, those to go in a box to move, and the ones two piles away that I can't reach should probably be tried on to know if they even still fit me.

I have a shirt halfway into a box when a sound catches my attention. A trilling tune that sounds really far away.

My phone! My eyes pop open, and I shove the clothes from my lap. My boot heels thunder through the house as I look on the table, the kitchen counters, in the bathroom. It is going to stop ringing if I don't find the stinking phone. Standing in the middle of the hallway, I look one way and then the other, straining my ears to pick a direction.

Head-first over the back of my brown chair, I shove my hands in the cushions. Ah, yep, found it. I clasp it in my hand, and it stops ringing. I right myself and stare at the device with slumped shoulders. All that work to be a hair too late.

The outgoing call rings send my heart beating faster, but it doesn't run away. I guess that's a start, but if there is such a thing, I'd really like to get to a place where making a phone call doesn't wind me up like a seven-day clock. I twirl a piece of hay that came out of the depths of the brown chair along with the phone.

"Hey." Ian's voice jolts me from my thoughts.

The hay drops from between my fingers. Rats! "Hey, sorry I couldn't find my phone." An airy laugh floats out between my lips. Well, that sounds pitiful.

Ian laughs. "Would you be able to help me work a few calves this Saturday?"

Saturday. That's like three days away. "Sure." I roll my eyes and look on each arm of the chair for the little pipsqueak that said that, but it's all me. When will I learn? Last time I said "sure," I ended up making a terrifying phone call. But then it hasn't turned out all bad.

"Great. I've got a handful I want to get done before they get too big."

A little smile plays its way onto my face. "Yeah, that sounds good. What time should I be there?"

"Ah, seven-thirty? They'll just be in a little trap."

"Sounds good." I retrieve the hay from the floor and perch on an arm of the chair. A pause turns into an awkward silence. "Should be daylight by then."

"Yeah, be able to see if it's a cow or a bush."

"Right." I twirl the hay. It's not office hours. I shouldn't ask him. But I don't have anything better to say, so... "You haven't heard anything on that lease, have you? As nice of a place as it is, I wouldn't think it would take long for it to be snatched up and Wade sure is taking his time deciding."

"Oh, no, that place isn't going anywhere." Ian clears his throat. "I mean, Wellman isn't that kind of guy. He knows Wade's serious."

My eyebrows knit together. What does he mean it isn't going anywhere? And then to cover himself? Ian never does that. But then how would I know? I've had, what, a half dozen conversations with him over two weeks? I slap a smile on my face, hoping it oozes into my voice too. "Good deal then."

"Well, I've got to get to the post office. I'll see you Saturday."

"See you then." Beep, beep, beep. I shake my head. *Well, that was strange.*

Have any of the stragglers calved while I've been playing house? I set my hat on my head; I need some fresh air, anyway. In the sunshine I feel my bones smile, and my airway instantly feels crisper. Amazing what being outside does and how little inside time it takes to suck it all away.

All five heifers lie around chewing their cuds. It draws a sigh out of me. Hurry up and wait. That's the story on just about everything right now. As much as I enjoy the spontaneity calving season gives life, I wouldn't mind if they quit their games and finished this up.

The birds flit from greasewood to an all-thorn bush and back again. Haygrazer dust drifts on the wind, tickling my nose into a sneeze. I lower myself to recline against the pipe fence. The packing can wait.

Chapter 9

Dune's nicker in the still morning air probably could have been heard a mile away. I pull around by the pens beyond Ian's house. Almost as soon as the slam of my pickup door behind me dies away, I hear hooves on hard ground. Leggins in hand, I turn to face a chipper Ian.

"Good morning, sunshine."

My face lights up, and a little giggle bubbles out. "Good morning." I pull my leggins on, buckling them up tight around my waist.

"Which one is that?" He flicks the ends of his reins towards Dune in the trailer before turning to tighten his cinch.

I drag a bridle from the passenger seat and straighten the reins as I say, "Dune; he's the five-year-old. Lessens the likelihood of an unplanned dismount."

He laughs over his shoulder. "You're the age to err on the side of making those dismounts happen."

I shake my head. "Nope. You've got to be ten feet tall and bulletproof for that stuff, and I am not."

Dune takes the smooth solid bit, moving his tongue against the copper roller, but a groan shows his protest when I tighten the cinch. leggins, bridle, cinch—

Ian's voice interrupts my mental checklist. "There's only a handful, so I figured the two of us could manage it."

I nod. "Sounds good to me."

Ian leaves his horse's reins draped over the fence by the gate into a long alley and weaves his way through the pens. With each step, the bottoms of his leggins flare like the anxiety in my chest. I hate watching other people work, but I have zero clue what would be helpful. He shuts a few gates and leaves a few others open.

Outside the alley gate, he squats down and starts drawing in the dirt. I move around to watch over his shoulder. Using the end of a stick, he makes an indention. "These pens are here. We'll go out down this west fence that corners and turns towards the north out here." He makes another indention. "The middle's pretty open, so we'll throw them out there and then bring them in."

"How big is it?"

He stands. "Section and a half."

A little grin slips to my face. That's the size of the heifer trap at home. I meet his gaze and catch a glitter of amusement. Oh great, no pressure.

On horseback, Ian sends me to the outside, which suits Dune and me just fine. Ears perked, Dune swings his head with each stride in his fast walk. Each step has a touch more pep in it until I squeeze my calf muscles against his sides and he takes off in a long trot. I alternate between checking the brush for cattle, keeping an eye on Ian's whereabouts, and staying the course of the fence.

Maybe a couple more blades of grass exist here then there are at home, but a couple is all. Ian is in as bad of shape as the rest of us. Mom's words from several months ago ring in my head: "Uncle Ian is working on growing his herd so he can back off of the real estate business." The shape this country is in sure isn't going to help him with that.

About the time I decide Ian has dropped off, I ride into the middle of a thicket and find two Hereford cows and three calves. The calves throw their tails in the air and leave out in a playful run. The cows follow in their calves' paths in a not-so-playful run.

Eyebrows touching my hat, I scoff, "Well, get out of Dodge, then."

Another cow with her half-grown calf trots down the fence. A moment later a catclaw thicket blocks not only the path but the view down the fence. Dune picks his way through one high step at a time. When we come out on the other side, there is neither hide nor hair of the pair.

Lovely.

I swivel my gaze back and forth, studying the brush for them. The farther I go, the more sweat wets my palms. Well, that's about right! The first time to work with, let alone for, Ian, and I lose cattle. I bite my bottom lip.

Dune takes a couple halting steps. I encourage him forward with a squeeze of my legs. He points his ears towards a thickly leafed mesquite. Maybe the pair brushed up. My fingers tap on my leggins with hope, but when a mule deer bounds over the fence in front of us, my shoulders slump. So much for that.

The rest of the way around the trap, I don't see a single bovine. Hopefully, Ian has a whole wad of them.

A mesquite thicket spans out in front of us, and Dune takes a tentative step forward. I drop my hand down against his neck and crouch below the oncoming branches. As soon as I raise my eyes, my hand comes up, stopping him. Ian's big bay is as sweaty as my sorrel and is halfway between a wide-eyed half-grown calf and a high-headed cow eyeing an exit from the herd.

My rigid spine relaxes into a comfortable slouch, and I touch my spurs to Dune's sides. Breath leaves my lungs in rhythm with his hoofbeats. Dune jumps a tasajillo bush, and the calf swivels its head in our direction.

Don't be stupid, you ignorant sucker.

I slide Dune around to face the calf just before it whirls and shoves its way between the cows into the middle of the herd. Breath still comes in heavy gasps, but relief washes over me.

After a moment, the cattle accept their fate and settle out of their nervous milling. I take this opportunity to glance at Ian from under my hat brim. He backs his horse a step and gazes over the top of the cattle down the cleared strip through the brush. Smoke doesn't seem to be coming from his ears, so that's a good sign. Maybe we haven't lost too many of them.

A cow starts down the clearing, taking the rest of the herd with her. Before I dodge a branch to the face, I catch sight of the white speckles down her sides. *You huzzy.* Good to know she made it to the herd.

Ian and his bay leap into the brush, coming out into the clearing several yards in front of the cow. I bring up the rear, darting back and forth, turning the calves that seem to have forgotten they have a mother at all.

Even with a few chases to turn a cow back, Dune's breathing has returned to normal by the time we get to the pens. As I latch the outermost gate behind us, my chest gathers with nerves again. Now Ian gets to watch everything I do. I've done this all a million times, though. It'll be fine. I look up from latching the gate at a broad grin from Ian. Willing myself to relax, I smile too.

"What do you think?"

Think. I think you really know what you're doing, and I don't want to screw up in front of you. "Think about what?"

"Just what do you think?" His hands rest on his saddlehorn, leaving loose reins draped down his horse's neck.

I let Dune step up to the trough next to the bay. "I think you might have one more blade of grass than I do."

Ian looks over his cattle milling about. "That would be about all. I'm in about the same boat as Wade, but how much feed I can afford is the only deadline." He chuckles that amused chuckle.

It is always either an amused grin or chuckle, or a very serious face, like he was two worlds away in thought. Does he have a middle ground?

"Anyway, I think it's a good start to a beautiful morning."

Breathing a little easier since I don't have to try and reply to the grim reality we face, I smile at him. "It is, isn't it?"

"Well, let's get them sorted."

These pens were clearly not designed for branding, but they work. We sort the cows off first. Then fill syringes with vaccinations, and get the branding iron heating in a propane flame.

"Will your horse hold a rope?"

Syringe in hand, I freeze. As sure as I commit Dune to anything, he'll prove me wrong. "He's usually pretty good about it."

Ian nods and starts pulling the pickin' string from the left leg of his leggins. "You want to heel them and work them? I'll flank and hold them."

Oh nice, I get to heel and work calves right under his nose. He can study every detail.

It's been a while since I've cut a calf and even longer since I've drug one to the fire. But it's all like riding a bike, right? "Sure." That four-letter S-word that has gotten me in more uncomfortable situations than a kid saying the *other* four-letter S-word.

I cinch Dune up tight, walk him in a circle, and tug the latigo again until the buckle slides in one hole tighter. Here we go! Without my leggins binding at my hip, I catch the stirrup even easier than this morning.

After I drop a couple coils off the left side of my saddle, I tie a half hitch around the horn of my saddle in another coil of rope. *God, please don't let this knot come back to haunt me.*

Tying on hard and fast hasn't been my thing since the first time I had a rope on a horse. I'd drug a calf to the fire and held it, but in the mess of my first time in that predicament, my horse's back foot stepped over the rope before it was off the calf. There was no blow-up, but I very plainly saw what could have happened, and it scared me just the same.

If I'm going to be getting off to work these suckers too, I can't be fussing with getting the rope tied off every time, though.

My arm is tight as I swing a big loop a couple of times. Deep breath. I direct Dune to the wad of calves in the corner, starting big swings again. Musically, the rope whirls through the air. One, two, three, it sails. Thumb up, grab, pull. The rope comes tight around both back legs of the calf, and he starts kicking. My right hand starts to take the rope to the saddlehorn, and then I remember. I'm not dallying today.

I pull Dune back until there is tension in the rope. In a flash Ian has the small calf down. Oh yeah, this is my part, where I get off my horse. *Get it together, Nora.*

I grab the syringe and put the shot in the loose skin under the front leg. Racing as if the whole thing is timed, I miss the needle with the white cap twice before I get it slid in place. Now for the fun stuff! I take my knife from its scabbard on my belt and put a swallow fork in the right ear. It's a heifer, so I don't have to sweat while Ian watches me fumble my way through castrating. Not yet.

I toss the syringe haphazardly toward the fence, hop into the saddle and step Dune forward, so that Ian can let the calf up with less recipe for a rope wreck. This is one of those moments I wish I had taught my horses to lead better. Then I wouldn't have to get on in such a hurry. Breath comes in puffs while a smile fights its way to my lips. This is fun; nerves, adrenaline, and all. Coiling my rope, I turn Dune around, catching sight of that grin on Ian's face and Denise standing at the fence.

Even as I throw the next loop, I know it is going to miss. *Dang weenie arm of a throw.* I keep my eyes focused intently on coiling my rope up.

I try convincing myself it is okay, not to worry about them watching. Second time's the charm. And it is, but this time with only one leg in the loop. I still grab the rope to dally, but I catch myself and keep the rope picked up until all the slack is out of it.

Both my arms and mind have gotten in the groove of things by the fourth or fifth calf. I stop trying to dally and start bailing off Dune as soon as Ian has the calf down. At some point in the works, Denise disappears from her quiet spot on the fence. By the time Ian turns the propane off and I let Dune's cinch out a couple notches, sweat soaks through the backs of both our shirts.

My arms and core muscles are tired, but the kind of tired I will smile about when I sink into my chair tonight. I tote the box with syringes and other tools into the barn.

Ian claps me on the back, wearing his wide grin. "You don't know what it means to me that you've come out to help me today, girl. It's not been the same the last several months." He looks at me for just a moment before throwing an arm around my shoulders. "You're one cool cat."

I give him a hug. It's all I have to give him. Words aren't my strong suit.

Chapter 10

With each long stride to keep up with Ian, I regret the extra taco I ate at lunch.

Ian slows at the gate, and I blow out a breath. As I walk through the gate he holds open, he smirks at me. "I don't schedule naps on this outfit."

I laugh. "I don't think a nap is what I need, anyway. I ate way too much."

"See, when you're here, I can slip by and not eat as much and still not get in trouble. You're the one that gets the pressure if enough food isn't out of the pans."

"Oh, gee, thanks!" I roll my eyes, but my lips lift upward.

"My pleasure." He holds another gate open. "I'm not going to do anything to the cows, so let's put the calves there with them and take them down to the water lot."

"All right." I head for Dune and cinch him up again. He groans in protest, having nodded off into a nap. "Sorry, bud." I give him a pat on the neck before swinging into the saddle.

I hear Ian's voice and turn Dune towards him to hear the rest of what he's saying. He says more, and then I see the phone against his ear. Good, I didn't miss anything important. I cross my wrists over the saddlehorn and study the setup of the pens. With the barn in the middle and three different pens to bring them in from, they're set up nicely for calving heifers.

Since we left the calves alone while we went to lunch, they have stopped bawling. Most of them lie against the fence, in the little bits of shade they can find. Only occasionally does a cow's bawl pierce the afternoon air.

Caught up in watching the little ones, I don't notice Ian on his horse until he's riding towards the calves, phone still to his ear. *Dadgum, pay attention to what you're supposed to be doing, Nora.* A spur against his side wakes Dune from his daze, and he sidles up to the gate. I swing it into the pen with the cows before working my way around the fence.

Typical calves: they wander in circles, too ignorant to go around the end of the fence to their mommas. I keep my monster noises to a minimum since Ian's on the phone. Finally, when a few cows come around the corner into the little pen, the calves follow them out. I pull the gate closed behind all of them. The chain around the gate is just long enough it will latch, but there is none to spare.

By the time I've got it latched, Ian is fumbling with the one on the other end, phone still against his ear. I shake my head. There's no reason I couldn't have gotten that. I guess that would be considered asking for help, though, and nobody around here does that.

I follow the herd to the gate, pushing up sore steer calves that Momma has walked off without. As soon as they are through, I grab the gate. There's no need for Ian to stand on his head and try to talk on the phone again.

"Yes, sir. Whatever you think; specifics are up to you." Ian's words mix with the screech of the gate latch. "I want him to have the lease if he wants it. No, there'll be another one that'll hold my cattle just as well." He chuckles, but it is not amused. "Maybe one day I'll be able to explain it to you, Wellman."

Slowly, I right myself in the saddle. I wasn't trying to overhear his conversation; it just went to my brain. I turn Dune into the middle of the pen and trot him in circles. But for the record, what *had* I just heard? *Lease, there will be another one, I want him to have it.* Ian didn't just give up a lease he had nailed down for his cattle, did he? *There's no way.* Breath catches in my throat. Not *that* lease.

He does know it so well, though. And a couple times when he talked about it, he stumbled over himself. My heart drops. Just this morning he had said he needed to find a place to put his cattle. That piece in Huntsburrow would be perfect for these girls.

My stomach churns. *Please let me be reading way too much into this.* I kick Dune into a lope and ask him for a lead change into a right-hand circle.

"What do you think?"

I lift my reins and Dune clatters to a walk. No. Not that question. Not now. "I, uh, I—"

Ian's eyes narrow.

Dadgummit. He's too good at reading me. I have to say something. "You didn't give up that lease, did you?" I pick at a nick in my reins.

His face loses color.

Dang it! Why did I have to hear anything at all? Then we could just have gone on with life none the wiser.

No, at some point it would have come out, and I'd hate myself for walking all over him like that. Ian's already given me too much, helping with the breech, feeding me multiple times, and no telling how many hours he's spent working on finding leases. I have to do something. But I have no idea what.

My fingers clamp around the reins. "Why would you do that?" My voice comes out softer and less desperate than I feel, thankfully.

His gaze goes beyond me to the cows in the water lot. "I-It's important that the next generation get in and stay in the business."

I just cock my head.

He shifts in his saddle and for a fleeting moment looks at me.

Breath comes shallowly. It's too much. No one gives up land for their long-lost niece. Nobody but Ian.

I touch Dune with my spurs, riding past Ian. There's so much to say, yet no way to say it. I step to the ground by the barn and throw the reins over the fence. A syringe still lies by the fence. I snatch it up and take it to the water trough. I've pushed one round of water through it and am filling it for a second round when I hear Ian's spurs jingling closer.

"You don't have to do that. I'll tend to them later."

I turn to him, and the words I had get stuck in my throat. A little green folded rectangle rests between his forefinger and thumb. I shake my head. "I'm not taking your money."

A puzzled look starts to form on his face, but then his shoulders just fall. "Nora—"

"You've already given me more than I can ever repay."

"What are you talking about?"

Tightness spreads across my chest like the spray of the last bit of water from the syringe I empty. "All the work you've done looking for leases, anyone else would have paid you for that. You've paid for my meals at least twice, helped me with that calf, and probably something else I'm missing. Relationships are give and take, and I'm doing all the taking. I don't want it to be that way."

A long sigh leaves his chest, and he perches a hip on the side of the trough. "Nora, anything I've given you can't possibly begin to pay on what you've given me."

"A headache?"

He shakes his head. "No." His hand raises a couple inches off his leg, then returns again. "These months since Kayla's car wreck have been hell. I can't get out of the *what-if* loop. What if I hadn't let her go to that concert? What if I had gone with her? What if, what if, what if." Slowly, he looks up at me. "Until that day I got your phone call. You're not Kayla. I wouldn't want you to be. But you filled a void. You've given me something to focus on that is present and positive. So again, anything I've given you can't start to repay what you've given me."

My throat bobs, and my brain can't form words.

"Does that all make sense?"

I nod. "Yes." It comes out so softly I'm not sure he hears me. "I'm sorry," I whisper and throw my arms around his neck.

Chapter 11

I crank the window up while holding my phone between my ear and shoulder. One, two, three, rings of the phone. The rush of wind into the cab is cut off, and I put my left hand back on the wheel just in time to keep it in my lane around the curve halfway home.

"Hey, Nora!"

I startle at Wade's upbeat voice, and then his voice is consumed into darkness, like the two ccs of Black Leg vaccine I gave the calves just a few hours earlier.

"Wade, have you signed the lease yet?" Wow, that was direct.

Question marks hang in his voice when he says, "No, I'll send it off in the next day or two."

I release a breath. If I were asking for any other reason, I would have rolled my eyes, but this time I'm thankful for his stalling nature. "Okay, good. I, uh, have a few things I want to bring up about the place." That sounded professional, right?

"I'll be coming over in the morning to look at the calves anyway. We can talk then."

Looking in my mirror, I scrunch up my nose at the car that won't go around. Calf checks, of course, are always a good reason for Wade to pop in. I lick my lips, swallow, and say, "Talk to you then."

Wade's parting words and the beeps of an ended phone call hardly register as one thought spirals through my mind.

What do I say to him?

Bring up a few things. What was I thinking? The place is practically perfect! Besides, I have been asking about a lease for the last three months, so if I come up too picky on this one, he might leave me high and dry and take it anyway. After all, I'm not indispensable. But I can't just say that my uncle gave it up and I don't want him to do that for me. That sounds like I'm a selfish child, anything but a capable young woman.

My throat is tight as I put the pickup in park and turn it off. I throw my hat on the dash, wipe my forehead with my arm, and lean my head back against the seat. Now what have I gotten myself into?

You have to do it. For Ian. It's sweet and nice, and I'm honored that I can help him through missing Kayla, but giving up a lease he needs isn't how I'm going to do that.

***

Supper wallows around my plate by the prodding of my fork until it is cold. My throat is too tight to allow much to go down, and even if it did, I'm not sure my stomach wouldn't send it back up.

There have to be other places to lease, other people I can call.

Leaving the fork still on the plate, I slide my leftovers into the fridge. I pick my hat up on my way out the door, only to spin it around one hand while I lean against the cement next to the back door.

The sun is on its way down. Snorts and groans of the heifers bedding down float on the breeze. Little birds make their final flitters of the evening. The world is at peace.

I, on the other hand, am somewhere between wanting to puke, having the flu, and being about to cry. Maybe all of them at once. I lean my head against the wall of the house and finger the worn brim of my hat.

Ian has lost so much. No amount of explaining will make it sit right with me. I can still be there for him even if Wade doesn't have that lease. Even if I don't have this job.

Pain mixes with tension and comes up my throat. Either way this goes, it isn't going to be fun. But this hasn't been fun for a while. It has gotten so much deeper than that, and in a hurry.

For the second night in a row, I don't sleep a wink. Flip, flop, and turn all night long. Halfway between my two and four a.m. night checks, I go out again, just to feel productive. Thankfully, one of the last two heifers is in labor. I have my doubts that the other one will calve at all.

I go back to the house and throw on some real clothes instead of watching the action in my pajamas. The anticipation puts sparklers in my fingers and toes. It happens every time. The thrill and wonder of a new life being brought into the world as I lean against the fence.

Of all the calves I've watched be born on this place, this might be the most special one. The last one. I sigh. It might be the last one I watch be born for a long time. I'll give this place up one thousand times over if I don't have to bear the weight of keeping Ian from his goals, his dreams. One day he is going to look back and regret letting it go because of a skinny kid who isn't always tough enough to take life dry-eyed. No, I'm not going to let that happen.

Compact, wet, and slimy, the new little calf wobbles into the world. His momma is quick to turn and lick him off, putting that unimaginable life into him. Within fifteen minutes he has his first taste of milk and is settled down under his momma's protective gaze. I hang out a while longer, relishing the comfort of the pair, that love that can't be broken by an outside force.

The peace of the night doesn't stick around much after daylight. At some point this morning, Wade will drive up, and I have to tell him something. The best I've come up with is that the gates are wire and shipping cattle back and forth will cost a lot. I don't really think that will hold him long, but it's the best I have except for the truth. Maybe by God's grace he'll be second-guessing it anyway.

Breakfast doesn't sound like a good idea, but I force down a couple slices of cheese and a couple dozen chips before heading outside.

Wade usually doesn't show up before ten, but I don't want to risk riding out to check the pairs and miss him. I drag out my saddle, a couple bridles, and an old bottle of olive oil. All my gear needs a nice dose of hydration, anyway. My thoughts slip through me the way the oil slips through my hands. What if Wade doesn't buy what I say? What if I have to tell him the truth? What if he thinks I'm a child? I stop halfway down a rein with the oiled sheepskin. What if he thinks less of Ian?

The saying that a watched pot never boils? Well, apparently a watched lane never brings a vehicle, either. For the third time, I take the sheepskin over the same section of bridle rein. A horse snorts, and the sheepskin falls in the dirt. I sigh. What am I even doing? Can't focus, can't think, can't even hold onto the sheepskin!

I pick it up and beat it against the saddle house door. Dirt flies, but not nearly as much as is stuck to the oily surface. Any bit of joy that remained in my gut is officially gone. If only I had just accepted my fate before, none of this would be happening. I sink back down on the five-gallon bucket I claim as a chair.

When Wade's Dodge finally does rattle up the lane, sweat breaks out under my hat. Thank goodness for small graces like a hat to hide it. I force myself to take a couple deep breaths while the pickup wheels are still rolling.

"Good morning, Nora. Is that a new little baby I see over there?"

Some things don't change. Take a deep breath; it's a blessing. "Yeah, it was born last night. I'm pretty sure it's a little bull calf. How are you this morning?" Looking over my shoulder at the calf, I wring my hands before stuffing them in my pockets.

Wade starts towards the fence, and I tag along behind. He leans up against it and cracks a little smile. "He's a cute little fella, ain't he? Last one?"

My eyes go to the last heifer that is supposed to calve. "That one over there is supposed to have one, but I'm not sure anymore. She doesn't seem to be bagging up. I haven't got her in the chute to check. I guess I need to." *Way to go, Nora. Stick your foot in your mouth already.*

Wade is grinning at me when I look up. "One out of seventy-five is pretty good in my opinion. What is it that you wanted to talk about? I'll look at the pairs on my way out."

My deep breath turns out shaky. I take my hands from my pockets, intertwining my fingers, then jerk them away and stuff them in my back pockets. "Just some things I noticed at the place. You know, we finally got most of the gates upgraded to nice swinging ones around here. I noticed a lot of those down there were tight wire ones." Wade makes no move to say anything, so I go on. "And I was just thinking about how far it is. I know how you like to keep up with how the calves are growing and the heifers are calving out and all of that. It'd be hard to make a four-hour drive just to check on things." I drive my thumbnail under the fingernail on my index finger.

Wade stares out at the half-eaten bale of hay grazer for a long moment, then slowly turns towards me. "Nora, you've been working for me years now, and not once have I sensed any reason not to trust you."

Breath hitches in my chest. *Uh oh.* Even under the protection of my hat brim I don't let myself squint.

"I don't see why four hours' distance is any reason to stop trusting you now. And I've been looking for a good writeoff for a while anyway. Fuel looks like a good enough one to me."

The positive words don't keep my shoulders from slumping. I force myself to paste on a smile before looking past my hat brim. "It's one the government shouldn't question, anyway."

Wade slaps the top pipe of the fence. "Darn right! Well, if that's all, I'll be looking at those pairs now. I should have the lease papers signed by the end of the week. But I'll probably be out of pocket after that. I'm thinking about heading down to Fredericksburg."

I nod and swallow. "Yeah, that was all. I'll–I'll talk to you later, then. Enjoy your trip." True to Wade fashion, I don't have to find anything else to say. As soon as the gray Dodge is turned around and headed back out the way it came, I sink down on the bucket. So that's it. It is a done deal.

Why don't I feel happy? This is just what I've been fighting for for months now. It doesn't feel right, though. It still feels as though I'm taking something from Ian, like it is not rightfully mine. One day he's going to come back and wish he hadn't done it. I sniff. He especially will if I keep letting salt water spill from my eyes.

I rake them away. *A rancher doesn't have time to cry.*

The whole rest of the day I see to just that. I finish my oiling project and ride out to see the pairs, going over every nook and cranny of the pasture to find the very last calf. Bypassing lunch, I put out hay next to the scattered remains of the last bales. Calves scramble from the mounds when I drive up. I take them several bags of cake too.

The weaned heifers get hay as well and a few less sacks of cake. I calculate and recalculate how long that will last them and if I will need to put out another bale before we ship. If I cake them more, they should make it on this hay.

Ian rings in the back of my mind like a song on loop. I focus on anything else. Once again, I have tried my best, and it isn't enough. I can't keep the land from being taken from under him. Once again, what I hold special is slipping through my grasp.

Chapter 12

Ring!

I pat the side table while trying to get the clouds out of my eyes. Something rolls off and clatters to the floor. Awesome. I flop over into cool sheets and squint against the daylight. My phone vibrates again, this time jarring me awake. I finger the cool device and turn it over. Reading the name across the top of the screen pops my eyes wide open.

I sit up straight in bed and swallow before tapping the little green circle, hoping sleep sounds further away than it is. "Hello."

"Good morning, Nora." Wade's deep voice is heavy, and he sighs. "I just got off the phone about that lease. Lightning caught it on fire last night and burned it. Wellman said they won't be leasing it out at all."

I suck in a breath, my heart dropping. *I guess it won't be helping anyone out of a bind now.* "Wade, I'm sorry. I know you were really excited about it." Gah, that sounds terrible, but what else am I supposed to say?

"It wasn't meant to be, I guess." He chuckles without humor, so unlike himself. "But that does put us back in a pickle and with not much time, either. In fact," he sighs again, "I think I'll go ahead and line up a truck for the end of this week. If we find something, I'll send them to the main ranch to hold them. If not..." He leaves it hanging, because he doesn't have to say it; we both know.

My heart now plummets down to my toes. It is real; it is happening. I have tried to avoid looking at the calendar, but Wade's words bring it clearly to the front of my mind. Two weeks, probably from today, are all we have. I run a hand over my face. "Yeah, that sounds good."

"I'll let you go. I just wanted to fill you in."

"Thanks for calling. Talk to you later. Bye."

Wade's parting words and the click of the phone line are like a yearling's kick to my gut. I hold the phone in my hand for a long moment before tossing it at the end of the bed. I lie back, staring at the flaking ceiling.

No need to worry about living on and working a piece of land, knowing Ian could have grown his herd there, now. This way Ian won't have anything to expand on either, though. And Wellman. What will become of him and the place?

Suddenly, it's not just my heart and dreams, but Wellman's and Ian's too. That nag of losing ranching and working the land comes back with vengeance, because it's not just for me—it is for them. And there is not a thing I can do to help them.

Not when I am talking about failed cotton for eight hours a day.

I force my legs over the side of the bed. My foot touches the rug there, but I jerk it back up at the sharp poke of a tiny prickly pear thorn. "Dadgummit."

Brushing my fingers over the bottom of my foot, I locate the thorn and rake it out of my skin. Today sure is getting off to a good start.

I kick the middle box in a stack of three boxes of kitchen things. *Stupid boxes. Stupid stuff. Stupid moving.*

From my bedroom the phone rings again, but I don't turn around. I put on a pot of coffee, letting the percolator drown out the ringing. My back is anything but straight, and my stomach has wadded up in a ball. It's like having the flu and a stomach bug at the same time, but this time sleep and Pepto won't help anything.

I try to think of what-ifs—things that could have gone differently—but really there are none. Lightning is natural; nobody but God could have stopped it.

God.

A shaky breath pushes back against the emotions rising in my throat.

If I knew it would come down to this, I would have prepared, been in the middle of a mesquite thicket. My head sinks against my folded arms on the counter and I swallow the lump. I've always been able to take the pain. Until it gets to that point and I can't. How much more will I have to handle? How much more *can* I handle?

The coffee pot beeps, and I slowly straighten. Even when the coffee makes a storm with the cream and the cup warms my hands, I feel cold. So empty.

A couple cups down and with one in my hand, I drag myself into some clothes. Refill the cup, pop a lid on top, and then go out to the barn. Each step feels like I'm lugging a bag of feed with me.

I rattle oats in a bucket until the three geldings come trotting into the pen. I feed them and the heifers that are still hostage.

When the horses are done, I get a bridle and catch the old man. He's actually in his prime, but compared to the other two, he's the senior. Banks follows me faithfully to the barn and cocks a hip while I saddle him.

Thankfully, he's shorter than Dune or Cante. I don't have the want-to to launch myself fifteen hands into the saddle. His steps are proud and swift, countering the weight I carry. He has no idea the life that's coming for him, and yet I can't get it out of my mind. Sharing a pen the size of my house with the other two in the middle of town, and if he's lucky a once-a-week ride down a county road. No, he deserves better than that.

The breeze plays with the wisps of hair that don't fit in a braid. Look at that. I don't have my hat shoved down against the wind. If any rain clouds were to gather, they might get a chance to drop some before getting blown on. I don't dare dream of the possibility, though.

Banks picks up a trot, sending a jackrabbit running from under a greasewood bush. A couple hundred yards ahead of us, two calves chase each other, tails high in the air. I plant my butt in the saddle and lean back a hair. Lifting the reins ever so slightly, I smile at Banks' smooth stop.

In their joyfulness, the calves buck when one mounts the other. The epitome of life right there.

Off to the left, in a little circle without brush, the newest pair I turned out stands. Mama chewing her cud, baby nursing with his tail wagging wildly. He hasn't quite lost his umbilical cord, but he hasn't had any trouble figuring out his legs.

I don't want to let go of the heaviness. It doesn't feel right; all this is going to be gone, but my lips just won't hold a frown. I relax into the saddle. This is it. The life I live for. A tear spills over and trails down my cheek. I lean down to pat Banks' neck.

The two-track road is just the other side of the pair. After watching them a moment longer, I point Banks to the road. Muscles now alive, I send him into a trot. Banks' ears erect and stride extended already, he takes off at the first hint that I'm leaning forward.

The wind we create dries out my eyes, and I reach up to push my hat a little farther down. Banks curves to the left with the road, and I sit back, reining him in from a run to a slow lope. His sides heave and nostrils flare, but he still doesn't want to slow down. I smile.

"I know, bud." It's me too.

We only do it for a bit before running into a yearling heifer and challenging her right out of the wrong pasture. Sun overhead, sweat down my back and dripping down Banks' legs, we both settle down a little after that. When I point him back to the barn, my mind starts running. Playtime is over; it's time to get down to business.

I can go to town to the feed store and ask Sam if he knows who owns the land outside of town that hasn't had a cow on it in five years. It's small, but it's something. There are definitely more people and more leases, but how I find them, I don't know.

***

Over a half-burnt bean burrito, I listen to a voicemail from Wade.

"Hey, I was just going to let you know I got trucks lined up. They'll be there Friday at eleven. Bye."

Comforting. I sigh. I've been fighting this for months, yet it has creeped in and taken root.

Reluctantly, I tap on the voicemail from Ian.

"Hey Nora, it's Ian. I just got off the phone with Wellman. Give me a call back."

I really don't want to talk about it, but somehow talking to Ian sounds nice. Comforting even. I stuff the last bite of burrito in my mouth and send a text to Wade.

I'll have them ready.

What I don't add is the broken heart I feel while typing the words. Sending my pride and joy off to the sale barn, where they will bring the insanely low price every other bovine is bringing these days. Yeah, that's nice.

The chunk of burrito I have been wallowing around seems to grow in my mouth before I finally close my eyes and will it to go down and stay there. I drink half a glass of tea before tapping Ian's name on my phone.

My knee drums in time to the ringing, and at his "hello," I have to clear my throat before answering.

His voice is extra soft when he says, "How are you?"

My knee still bounces. "Ah, well, my brain is running so fast my body can't keep up."

There is a pause. "What are you thinking?"

My shoulders slump. "I don't know. Wade's got trucks coming Friday. He says he's gonna look for another place." Under my breath I add, "He doesn't sound like he has much faith in anything coming from it."

I hear Ian's office chair squeak through the phone. "With all his specifications, there's only a couple options in a million."

My lips twitch up grimly. Sugarcoating isn't a strong suit of Ian's, and I'm glad. False hope is worse than no hope. "Yeah, and we're running out of time. I keep trying to think of an option we've overlooked, but so far I haven't come up with anything." I chuckle dryly. "Papercuts aren't so bad, right?"

His chuckle matches mine. "Don't resign yourself to the desk so fast. I'll keep looking too." He inhales deeply. "If it comes to that, why don't you just move in with us? To tide you over. I've got a couple extra bedrooms, and you can throw your horses in with mine. I'm sure we can wrestle you up some day work and colts to start until you find what you're looking for."

Words, if I had any, would have stuck in my throat. Move in with Ian? Burden him? He's already done so much. How can I possibly ask him for that? "Thank you. Maybe I won't have to, but if I do—I don't finish because I don't know how to. I don't know how to tell him all the appreciation that's in my heart for him. "Thank you," I whisper.

Silence carries the line before I ask, "How is Wellman?"

"He's doing all right. The kids have already started using this as another reason he needs to move in with one of them, but he's set on staying. There'll be enough clean-up work to keep him entertained."

I crack a smile. "He sounds like he'll get his kids persuaded."

My phone beeps against my ear, and I pull it away. What does that noise mean, anyway? Oh, yeah, that's the interrupting call one. "Hey Ian, James is calling me. I gotta go."

"All right. Let me know what you need."

"I will, thank you." I have to stare at the options at the bottom of the screen a moment before I end that call and accept the other one. "Hello."

"Hey, Nora, uh, Wade called me this morning."

"It's all right, James. Somehow, it'll all turn out all right." Once the words are out of my mouth, I realize how stupid they sound, but at least James doesn't have to feel stupid tiptoeing around the topic.

"Well, I'm glad you're not too down about it." That dry humorless chuckle that everybody has been giving me comes out of James too. "I was afraid I might have to come tail you out of a ditch or something."

My chuckle is not humorless. The picture his words paint in my mind is so embarrassing I can't help but laugh to shake it off. "No, not quite, but if you're available, I might take some help loading a truck on Friday."

"Wade's already got a truck?"

I narrow my eyes and cock my head. "I thought you said you already talked to him."

There's a tapping sound like a pen on wood. "I did, but he didn't say anything about shipping."

"That's funny, because if Wade roots up a lease, you're going to be hanging out with all these girls for a couple weeks."

"You learn something new every day!" He clears his throat. "I've been fighting water for several days now and I'm still not sure I got it running, so as long as I don't have water problems, I'll be there."

"Well, that sounds like fun." The moment laspes, and I pick up the napkin by my plate. I begin folding it back and forth, waiting on something to magically pop into my head to say, but for once I'm not panicking about it.

"So, um, Nora, how are you really doing?"

My hand stops folding, and I look up. How am I really doing? "Well, being mad about it doesn't change anything. I've had enough time to think about it and decide it won't kill me."

James sighs. "Dang it, I hate this."

Don't we all.

Chapter 13

A wiry mesquite limb smacks my cheek. "Dadgum." I blow the words out between gritted teeth.

Five yearling heifers book it down the fenceline, wanting no part of captivity. There's always at least one rebel in the bunch. Fifty-eight of their friends are already secured in the trap, thankfully.

Cante's mane flares away from his sweaty neck as he jumps a tasajillo bush. We have stop-started our way up and down this fence line three times already, but even with their tongues hanging out, these girls are having none of it.

"Stupid kids," I mutter, poking my spurs against Cante's sides. We've got to *go*. There's a dirt tank coming up, and if we don't get them turned before it comes, we can kiss the heifers goodbye. The finality of this gather must have gotten in their blood and set them on being a problem. Either that, or it's the pressure breathing down my own back.

Leaning down, partly to avoid another branch, partially to encourage Cante, I poke his sides again. *Two more strides, buddy.* He stretches out his stride once before breaking into the middle of a cedar thicket. He jolts to a trot, and I bring my hand up. Sides heaving and wind whistling through his nostrils, he stops.

My shoulders sag. *Well, that sucks.*

I lean down and pat his sweaty neck. "You did good, bud."

One step at a time, we weave through the cedar to the other side of the thicket and watch the little trail of red bovines still trotting down the fenceline in the wrong freaking direction. I shake my head. "They don't even know what stopping is."

Even with the walk to the house, Cante is still dripping sweat when we get there. I keep him walking in circles around and around the barn until his breathing gets back to normal. When I have unsaddled him, I lead him around the corner of the barn and hose him off. He doesn't even skitter around to get away from the stream. I fill my belly with water from the hose too.

When I turn him loose in the pen, he immediately goes to the corner with soft dirt to roll, then squeezes into the shade with the other two. I hang the hackamore up in the barn and sink onto the step. All that water I drank sloshes around, mixing with the heat radiating from my face to make for a queasy feeling. I take my hat off and wipe my face on my shirtsleeve.

With the pen from my leggins pocket, I write 58 on the palm of my left hand. The last five to go on that count will probably have to be treated for nylon deficiency. Maybe James and I will go rope them first thing in the morning.

I sigh. The pairs aren't gathered yet either, and trucks will be here to haul them out in a little over twenty hours.

If this dang ocean would stop spinning around in my stomach, I'd take Dune and get the pairs in.

I slog my way to the house and melt into the brown chair. The ceiling fan stirs the air, chilling my sweaty shirt. A hundred degrees in the shade is officially here for the season. I pull the blanket from the back of the chair and fold my arms under it.

There are too many pairs to stay in the calving lot, so I'll have to move the yearlings in there. It makes my head spin trying to figure out who needs to be sorted where and how to work everyone around in this set of pens. It's probably a good thing I won't have any more help than James. No more room than there is in these pens; they'd just be in the way. With the two of us, it will be slow sorting, though.

I cover my eyes with my hands and blow out a long breath. I guess if the truck has to wait on us, it just has to wait. Truck lights glow in my mind, and my chest tightens. Tomorrow is going to be one heck of a day.

I have done what I can to keep it from happening. Now I just have to cowgirl up and deal with it.

I nibble a couple of crackers before heading out into the heat again. Even if the ocean has settled down, food is about the last thing that sounds good.

After one cutting match with Dune, he stands in the corner to let me catch him. I put a dry though worn-down set of blankets on his back. Before swinging onto him, I take a couple small slurps of water, careful not to overload again.

Most of the cows have their calves laid out under the mesquites around the hay bale. Dune and I start them toward the gate I left open, and I get a rough count before riding farther into the pasture. At each water trough, I push groups out of the shade and start them on a slow walk in the sun.

The third time I have to go back to a bush and start the littlest calf again, I just get off.

"Look, small fry, I don't want to be out here in the dead heat any more than you do. Just get up there with your momma and go on." I slap it on the butt, but the outburst does little for the weight in my chest.

The calf bawls, and a cow turns to it. She smells the little one, turns, and calls to it as she walks off. Trotting to catch up, the calf bawls again.

I finger a piece of Dune's mane. The innocence of childhood. It's what I love most; it is my job to protect and nurture it. But it is what has hurt me the most too. It was the innocence that made me cry that night all those years ago that got me so fascinated with birth. The night I watched Muffin, the heifer calf I had raised on a bottle and hand-fed cubes, have a stillborn calf. I had waited two years for that calf; it was going to be the first calf to kick off my own little herd. The day I lost Muffin's calf, I cried big ugly tears with snot dripping, until all I had left were dry sobs.

"Facts of life," Dad told me. "Wipe your tears, now; there will be another one." And then he walked away.

I let a tiny smile quirk one edge of my lips. Yeah, there's been another one. Another couple hundred more.

The cow in front of me sniffs her baby and walks off, humming low to her little one.

Muffin's painted Corriente hide pops up in my mind even clearer now. Her calf would have been a heifer with splotches of white so much like her momma's.

The Hereford calf trots to keep up with his momma. I roll another piece of Dune's mane between my fingers. Now is not the time to cry over old memories. I've lost some calves in the last three years, some cows too, but for every one that isn't perfect, there's been ten that have been. Since Muffin, I haven't shed a single tear over a cow or calf either.

Now tears squeeze my throat. I swallow, but it doesn't take them away. Every day since that day, I've been damming those water works, and there's no reason to give in now. An awful lot has been pulling at them the last week, though.

Dune stumbles, causing me to focus my vision ahead. The glow of the barn light is fuzzy against the dusky sky. A drop of sweat falls from my hair onto the back of my hand. Gahlee, it should not be this hot this late.

The lead cow picks up a swinging trot towards the pens. The still evening sends the yearlings' calls drifting back to the herd. It draws a growl from my stomach. Food and sleep will put the waterworks in their place.

Half the herd is in the gate when the leaders start coming back out, bawling for their calves. Calves bawl back, some going through the gate, others drifting down the fence. Dune's ears perk up, and his steps are quick as he goes from one side of the drag to the other. The cows bunch up in the gate, leaving a wad of calves just outside of it.

Amazing. Just what I've always dreamed of happening.

I take my rope down and put a big loop in it, swinging low behind the calves. I slap one and then another on the back with it. They hump up and push amongst the group.

"Come on, cows," I growl.

The longer the madness goes on, the louder the cows bawl. A cow slips by, heading down the fence towards a calf. I'm already going to have to clean up this bovine mess; might as well let it go. I give Dune slack in the reins and push him into the big middle of the herd. "Shht, shht, shht, come on, girls!"

I turn Dune back out and slip around the left to turn a cow headed back into the depths of the pasture. "Goodnight, girls, go through the freaking gate." Dune lays his ears back and turns on the speed. When I pull him up, he turns towards the pens, ears up, and nickers a little. I follow his attention to a horse and rider bouncing towards us.

"Need some help?"

I bite my lip. Do I look like I need help? Of course I need help.

James' white teeth shine in the fading light.

"What are you doing out here?" I look over at him as he comes up on my right side. "On my horse, bareback."

"I came over to talk to you and saw you having trouble." He shrugs and moves up on Banks' back. "He looked gentle enough to do it on."

I shake my head. "Let's get these things penned."

With two of us, we get all the bases covered and all the cows and calves through the gate with only a few cups of sweat being spilled. James closes the gate behind the herd, and we ride through the bawling mass.

I open and close the last gate from Dune's back and have him carry me all the way to the barn door before swinging my leg over the cantle. My muscles tingle as I stand, and I lean against Dune a moment.

"You ready for the truck in the morning?"

Like a match to a short fuse, the words ignite a war inside me. I unbuckle the back cinch. "Nope." I don't mean it to pop out so harshly, but it's too late to take it back now.

James puts the cinches up on the off side of the saddle, and I pull it off, laying it in the dirt. As I turn to lead Dune to the pen, James stops me with a hand on my arm. I don't look up at him.

His hand drops, and he rubs it against his other one. "The main pressure tank busted at the house; I've got to go get one from Crane first thing in the morning."

My shoulders fall. What more can possibly go wrong?

"I'm sorry, Nora."

"It's okay." I push air out between my teeth. "I'll—I'll just have to call someone else." I rotate the faucet until the water pours from the hose.

For real though, God, how much do you think I can handle at one time?

"Do you have everything you need? I mean like Hot-Shot batteries and stuff?"

I close my eyes and swallow. "I don't have a clue." The words come out high-pitched, and my voice breaks at the end. Leaning over to turn the water off, I'm not so sure water won't leak out my eyes. I don't know how I am going to get these cattle sorted tomorrow, let alone if there are even Hot-Shots on the property.

"Here, I'll put them up," James says, closing his fingers around Dune's reins.

"Thank you." I wiggle out of my leggins, and hang them in the barn before hauling my saddle onto the rack. James hands me the bridles, and I hang them on a peg.

I turn to step out the door and nearly collide with James. He holds two boxes of Hot-Shot batteries toward me. "These should get you by."

A tired smile lifts my lips. James, of all people, being prepared. "Thank you. I'll leave them here so I can find them." I place them on a stack of feed before actually stepping out of the barn door.

"I'm sorry about leaving you in the lurch, but it's too hot..." He trails off.

I nod. "I know. Don't worry about it." I look towards the house and then his pickup that we stand in front of. "Well, I'll—"

"Yeah, I'll see you. Have a good night."

A sigh leaves my chest, and I'm thankful it's drowned out by the squeak of his pickup door.

So much for that bed that's been calling my name. I have a lot to get in order and about fourteen hours to do it.

I have to see this through.

***

In the house I grab my phone and find the contact I've been using quite a lot over the last several weeks. My heart doesn't run away as the phone rings. Maybe it is too tired for that.

"Hello." Ian's voice is smooth over my frazzled nerves.

"Hey, are you busy tomorrow?"

"Uh, no, what's up?"

I take a deep breath. "Well, Wade has trucks coming for the cattle in the morning. James was supposed to help me, but he's got to deal with water issues tomorrow."

"What time do you need me to be there?"

Breath comes easier. "Thank you! Six-thirty should be early enough."

Chapter 14

Damp air touches my face as soon as I step out the door. *Well, it's here. The day I've been trying to avoid.* I turn up the collar of my blue jean jacket and stuff my hands in my pockets. Head down against the breeze, I only look up once the rocks of the road fade into what wants to be grass.

The yearling heifers have yet to stir, and only a few momma cows stand, letting their calves nurse. I look out beyond them, and a smile breaks out on my face. Lined up on the fence are those five renegade yearlings. "Thank you, Lord," I murmur under my breath. I almost jump up and down. This day might turn out to be better than I thought.

I reroute to the barn for a bag of cake. The cows get to their feet and mob behind me as I string it out in the lot. I grab another bag from the barn and do the same with all but a quarter of it. Slowly, on edge, trying not to spook the youngsters, I make my way to the gate. Just as I am about to unlatch it, they jump up and trot off, but the rattle of the sack calls them back. Swinging the gate in, I drop the cake in a line just inside of it. A couple cows amble over, and at the same time four of the yearlings step through the gate. The other passes it with a jump to the side, as if it will bite her.

I clamp my lip between my teeth. "Come on." My muscles itch to move, but I hold them back. *Patience.*

The white bald face glows in the dim morning light. She stretches out her nose and sniffs. That's it. She sticks her tail in the air and hops through the gate posts, rushing up amongst her companions. I let out a breath, smile on my face, and do a hop of my own while pushing the gate closed.

There's a chance we'll have those cattle ready to walk on that truck at eleven after all.

When Ian pulls up, I sit atop Banks, setting gates up to move the cattle through. The horizon shines golden with a hue of pink. If a cow walks up a couple hundred yards from me, I can't tell you if it's a cow or a tree, but hey, maybe we won't be behind when the truck comes.

I close the last gate and ride up to Ian's trailer right as his horse steps out of the end of it. "How are you this morning?"

Ian looks up. "Just fine, and you?"

I step off Banks. "Well, my last five showed up at the gate, so I'm doing a lot better."

Ian gives me a hug with a tight grip and one final squeeze.

On horseback, we sit looking over the pens full of cattle. "So, there are five pairs and one that never calved that need to go with the yearlings. Then sort the calves off." Saying it out loud makes all the anxiety I've felt over it sound really stupid. Ian's probably done twice as much sorting in half as much time on multiple occasions.

"Sounds good."

Any grass that was trying to grow in that alley gets trampled in the first five minutes under the hooves of the yearling heifers going into a pen at the end. The heifer that never calved sorts out pretty easily and trots down the alley with them. The pairs are not so willing.

Once I have one paired up, the cow leaves the herd, but the baby runs back into the thick of it. Then by the time I have the baby back on the edge, the cow has already gone around the other side. After the third time, I pull Banks up and let a deep breath calm me.

They are cattle; fifteen-hundred-pound balls with minds of their own.

The first pair has finally edged out of the herd together when Wade's gray Dodge blows smoke and dust in our faces. My heart beats a little faster, but I turn Banks back into the herd and set my mind on work again.

The fifth pair trots down the fence to the pens, and Wade walks up the opposite fence.

"Ian, do you mind taking these up the alley?" I don't wait for him to answer before turning and trotting to meet Wade halfway. Hopefully, he doesn't ask many questions; my brain is too cloudy for that.

"Is that all of them?"

Breath momentarily refuses to go in my lungs. All of them? Every last one? "I believe so."

"Why don't we cut a little deeper? I need to be selling, not stocking the other place." Wade crosses his arms across his chest and surveys the pairs.

I look over my shoulder into the herd. "Sure, how many more do you want to cut?" *And how about you choose, because they're all running together for me.*

Wade studies a moment before taking several steps forward, stirring the herd up. I keep Banks a step behind Wade. He has not been feeding these hungry things. They'll run flat over anyone just to see if there's something in their pocket worth eating.

Pointing as he ambles through, he picks out fifteen pair that he wants to keep. All that cutting for nothing. Oh, well.

I send Banks into a lope, and we glide into the pens to intercept Ian. "So," my lips cock to one side, "Wade has decided he only wants to keep fifteen pair."

Ian chuckles. "That's classic. So we need these back?"

Under my hat I roll my eyes. "It looks that way." Ian starts to ride off. "Well, actually." I touch Banks with my spurs. "Why don't we just stick them in this little pen by the chute?"

Two cattle trucks create a dust billow that drifts towards the pens. I watch it come closer, and with it, the fate of my heifers. Banks jumps in front of a calf to the left, and I find myself halfway out of the saddle. My spur catches the billet of the back cinch as I grab for the horn, jerking myself back in place.

Get it together, Nora.

Banks pivots to the right and slaps his tail twice. Two cows slip between him, and the gatepost. He turns in behind them, and a couple more go by on the other. The dust clears and Ian drives a little bunch to us. This time I sit square in the saddle and pay attention.

The last cow slips by. I slap my hand against my leggins and shoo the calves back from the gate. Then I pull it closed. I feel the finality.

Wade motions me over. "We'll load out the yearlings first." He looks over at the truck driver perched on the chute. "How many do you want in the nose?"

Breath comes heavily, but I am grateful for instructions. I have to keep going—doing—or I'll lose it.

Numbers clatter around in my head. How many need to go in the next compartment, estimated weights of the cows and calves, figuring how many will be left for the next truck.

The second cattle truck is half full, and we still have a pen full of cattle. Maybe we'll have to drag this out into tomorrow. I push up another bunch for the next compartment and spot another cloud of dust coming up the lane. James comes rattling up with a forty-foot gooseneck tied onto the pickup.

We load thirteen calves in the front compartment and five of the littlest in the nose of the trailer. Their mommas squeeze into the rest of the trailer, so tight the gate barely closes.

James ties a pickin' string around the gates and winces. "Are you sure you want them so tight?"

Wade looks down the length of the trailer. "They don't have much room, do they?"

I step back to open the gate down the alley.

"Ah, let me hook onto that twenty-four over there. We'll split them up."

As soon as Wade is out of earshot, James says, "Thank goodness. Those girls don't have room to breathe." He opens the left trailer gate, and Ian gets the right one, careful not to let the flood come out too fast. They manage to get the flow shut off with something like a third of the cows out.

A few minutes after James pulls his rig out of the way, Wade backs in his place. The trailer hitch squeaks against the ball of his pickup with every uneven roll of the tires. Ian waves him back, making a fist with his hand, millimeters before the trailer touches the pipe of the alley gate.

The cows are hesitant to climb on another trailer, turning circles with their horns clinking together in the middle of the mass. Wade hands me a Rattle Paddle over the fence, calling me out of my daze.

You can do it.

I climb up on the fence a step or two to tap a cow in the front with the paddle. If it does anything, it makes them mill tighter. With a few more taps and several minutes for them to get their minds working again, the cows push one another on the trailer. Ian and James close the gates behind them. The latches sound like the hammer of a judge ruling in court. I tie a piggin string around the butterfly gates.

As I look through the bars into the trailer, my throat tightens up. I lock eyes with #94. The lack of appreciation for all the work I did pulling her calf still rests in her eyes. *So long, girl. Be sure your next baby daddy is a little smaller.*

"All right, we're out of here." Wade puts a hand on my shoulder. "You don't have to be in a big hurry to get moved."

I spare a glance at his face. His eyes look for anything except mine to focus on. I nod, because words won't work right now.

James is next, pulling me into a brief hug. "Tell me when you're moving, and I'll come help you out."

I feel a salt water drop on my cheek just before he pulls back and pats my shoulder with a tight smile. He walks away to his rig, and I wipe away the tears. They're all leaving. Probably better. I can go have my breakdown in the bushes that way.

As they start down the lane, I raise one hand hip-high in a pitiful wave. I feel the rattle of the trailer over the cattle guard as if I'm in the trailer. The yellow sidelights flicker like the moisture in my eyes.

Ian is still here. I can't do it now.

Later. I bite my lip. I need to go unsaddle Banks, but my boots have grown roots to the ground. Watery mucus drips from my nose, and I sniff it away.

Dang it.

I steel my muscles and wipe at my eyes. "Well, I guess that's all. Thanks for your help." A glance in Ian's direction is all I can manage. Maybe, just maybe, he hasn't heard the tears in my voice.

"Are you sure you don't want me to hang around? I don't mind."

I shake my head. "No, I'm fine."

Tension grows in my eyebrows. *Just hang on until he leaves, and then you can fall apart.*

The main gate by the chute squeaks. Ian stands at the end of it waiting for me, a sympathetic smile on his face. I swallow, but a hand grips my throat, the hand of tears.

I paste a smile on my face and go through the gate. How much more do I even have left to lose? My vision blurs. Great.

Banks switches the leg he has cocked as I approach. When he's between Ian and me, I lean against the gelding and breathe in his sweet smell. It fills my lungs, and I choke on it. A little cough and I spit out the snot that threatens to run down my throat.

"I really don't mind helping you. I don't have anything going on today."

That wasn't a break in his voice, right? Just in my hearing.

"No, thanks though." My voice *does* break. "That's all."

He gives me a hug that I half heartedly return before he leads his horse to the trailer.

Maybe he didn't hear the crack in my voice or see the water in my eyes.

I lean against Banks until the rattle of his trailer is louder than the purr of his pickup. Then I sink into Banks' shadow, and the tears are anything but contained.

Chapter 15

No heifers close to calving, leaving me in suspense; no new babies to keep an eye on; and no next year to anticipate. Is this what it will feel like every morning before going to a desk full of papers?

Is this what it feels like to accept defeat?

One, two, three, four breaths.

Defeat, defeat, defeat.

I swing my legs off the bed and shove my feet into my worn Twisted X shoes. I don't accept defeat. I haven't yet and ain't about to start.

First things first. I put a pot of coffee to gurgling. Then I go hunting for my favorite jeans and baby blue button-down. Dressed, I return to the kitchen just as the coffee finishes. With a buckskin-colored cup of coffee, I stir bacon into a skillet of eggs and warm a tortilla straight on the burner. All this food could easily feed three people, but I eat every last bite.

The boxes that have been haunting me feel a couple pounds heavier as I carry them out the front door. I clear the living room of boxes before sitting on the porch and leaning back against the house. I finger my hat brim.

The heifers are gone. I won't be putting low-birth-weight bulls with them at Christmas. No watching out for scours or even hacking brush out of a couple miles of fence this summer. I don't know exactly what I will be doing, and maybe that's the worst part.

Salty warmth runs down my cheeks. Ian probably already saw me cry yesterday. If he sees more tears, he'll think I'm not cut out for this work after all.

The curse of weakness comes down my cheeks again, and I shove it away with the calloused pads of my fingers. A leaf blows up beside me, and I crunch it in a fist. My heart is scrunching like my squinting eyes, and my chest shakes. There is no holding it back. The tears won't stop racking my body.

Not only did I not find a place for the heifers to go, but I've opened a whole can of worms that's liable to land me in that crop insurance seat after all. Cowboys aren't supposed to cry. Ian isn't going to want a weakling who isn't cut out for this hanging around.

I draw my knees up and rest my head against them. Between hiccups, my hearing grabs onto light footsteps. When I look up into Ian's gaze, my eyes dart away. I don't want to see the disappointment.

His boots scuffle against the wooden planks of the porch. I steel my muscles and watch him drive away in my mind's eye. Instead, the steps get closer, and his arm drapes around my shoulders.

Slowly, as if he will vanish if I look too quickly, I lift my head.

What is he doing? No one touches while tears fall. Wipe the tears, smile and carry on as if nothing is wrong, then maybe they knock my hat off and laugh as they go by.

I try to stop crying, but it only turns into hiccups. My brain can't come up with something to say even if my throat would allow me to.

Finally, I settle down enough to speak between gasps of air. "I'm—I'm so sorry. I'm not as strong as you thought I was."

Ian shifts to look at me head-on. "What do you mean?" His voice is soft like a slicked-up horse's neck.

I drag my forearm across my face. "I cry." A sob enforces that statement.

Several more sobs fill the air before I can say more. "I'm not tough enough to take the losses with a stone face." I sniff. "I break."

He reaches up toward his own eye, swiping at the corner of it. "It's not—" He sighs. "You have to be tough enough to cry. Anyone can shove things down and get mad and sull up."

I lift my gaze to meet his. Unfolding my legs, I lean over and wrap my arms around him. "Yesterday—" I swallow. "You left in a hurry." That wasn't entirely true. I'd practically begged him to leave. But it is out there already, can't take it back now.

His Adam's apple bobs on the top of my head. "I couldn't stick around because—" he takes a deep breath. "Because watching you watch those trucks leave felt a lot like watching Kayla's casket leave all over again. A whole world carted off like an Amazon package."

My shoulders slump, and another tear runs down my nose. Kayla. I've been so caught up in my own feelings, it hasn't even crossed my mind that Ian might be having some of his own. "I'm sorry."

He squeezes me in a tight hug.

Leaning back against the house, I pick up another mesquite leaf and pluck the petals off one at a time. "Thank you for being here." I fold a petal back and forth. "Really, it should have been my parents, but I'm glad it's you." I lick my lips. "I didn't really know what having an uncle or a friend was all about until two months ago."

"Thank you," he says, a little raspy, and hugs me tight again.

After several minutes of sitting in silence, Ian says, "Well, should we get you loaded up?"

"I don't know if all my house stuff is going to fit in my trailer, and I'll definitely have to come back for my horses."

He looks from my sixteen-foot trailer to the thirty-two-foot trailer on his pickup. "I think we can get it all, and if not, it's just one more trip."

I swipe dirt and grass from my jeans. "Are you sure you don't mind me couch surfing for a bit?"

"Denise will string your hide and mine both if you stay on the couch." He puts a hand on each of my shoulders. "We have plenty of room. And it will be nice having a youngin around again."

I smile. Maybe I can be more of a help than a bother to them.

***

The trailer gate touches Cante's back left hoof as Ian pushes it closed. Everything is loaded. Horses to kitchen forks.

The gate latches, and Ian puts a hand on my shoulder. "Well."

I look up and note the little beads of sweat circling down the side of his face. "I'll be behind you here in a few minutes." I look at the house. The house I'd grown into an adult in.

"See you in a bit."

With a side smile, I watch his pickup pull my horses and belongings away. When he stops at the highway, I turn back to the house. My hands clasp together in front of me. I take long steps towards the old house. "Well, God, this is it." I turn around to look out at the pens, where I've forced so many heifers to take their babies, where I've pushed my way through things I didn't know how to do. "Thank you for letting me grow here." The words get choked off by a sniffle.

Stepping inside the house, I breathe in the dirt and old wood mixed with droppings the rats have left behind. The place really will become their home now. At my bedroom I pull the door closed, and the one to the bathroom too, just like I always did before I went somewhere overnight. At the back door, I pull it hard and keep walking.

In my pickup, I focus ahead, determined not to linger on the goodbye. I don't look in the rearview mirror. Whether there would have been a new lease or not, I knew I had to say goodbye to this place, but it doesn't make it easier. Three years in that place is hard to let go of.

I have all the non-essentials in my trailer, so before heading out to Ian's, I stop by the self storage units in town. Sweat rolls down my back as I pull one piece of furniture out at a time. I am thankful to do it alone, if for no other reason than not to have to explain why I restack a pile of boxes three times.

I haul the last kitchen chair in, and when I come back out, James' pickup is pulled up. Rolling down the storage unit door, I put the lock in and try to think of something to say.

He stuffs his hands in his pockets. "I thought I told you I'd help you with that?"

A guilty smile spread on my face. "Ian came over and helped."

James nodded. "Good, you don't need to do that alone." He rubbed the back of his neck. "Nora, I'm glad you're not quitting the country."

I crack a smile. "Not yet."

He looks down and taps a gravel rock with the toe of his boot. "Uh, if you ever want to come out and ride or feed or whatever, you're welcome to. I mean, I don't know what your plans are or anything, but I just thought I'd offer."

"Thank you, James. I appreciate that." Now I am the one playing with a rock. "I'll be around for now. I'm going to be out with Ian and Denise."

"Good, I'm glad to hear it." He shuffles his feet and then looks up at me. "Well, that's all I stopped to say." One hand lifts in an awkward wave, and he strolls back to his pickup.

I giggle to myself and double-check the lock on the storage unit door. It's fun seeing someone else nervous for a change.

Chapter 16

After I wake up for the third night check I don't need to make, I start a pot of coffee in Ian and Denise's fancy pot. Bunn doesn't take ten minutes to brew coffee; about two minutes and I am slipping out the back door with a mug in hand.

In the distance I see the horses' silhouettes, my three already accepted into the herd's pecking order. They've whipped a few of Ian's young ones to get those places in the rank.

I might not have been able to keep the heifers from being sold, or get Ian his lease back, but there might still be a way that I can help.

The door squeaks, bringing my lips from the mug right before the coffee reaches them. I smile, but don't move to get up from my perch on an old stump. "Good morning."

Ian finishes his drink of coffee. "Good morning. You look deep in thought. Sorry I interrupted."

I shake my head. "No need to be." Before taking another sip, I wrap both hands around the steaming cup. "Have you heard any more from Wellman?"

If Ian was a horse, his ears would have swiveled forward. "Not a whole lot. I know his kids have really been badgering him to move, but his mind hasn't budged an inch."

A little smile cracks my lips. I can understand that. "I've been thinking..." I roll my lips around. How to say this...

Ian leans against the house.

"I think I'd like to go see him." I look up into Ian's face. His arched eyebrows push me onward. "I think it's pretty cool that he's so set on staying, even at his age."

A grin lights up Ian's eyes. "They'll have to drag him off that place before he leaves." He shakes his head. "Not many made like him these days."

I nod. "Would you write me some directions to his house?"

***

I look again at the map Ian drew me. Siri probably doesn't even know these dirt roads exist, much less how to get someone around on them.

How much further does this dirt road go before the S-curve? He did say it's past the S-curve, though. You're on the right road. Was Ian going to call Wellman? How awkward if not!

But who am I kidding? Either way, it is going to be awkward.

Right curve, left curve, straight. I slow down, watching for a house or a turn off. The tin peak of the house shines in the sunlight, and breath comes a little easier. I am in the right spot anyway.

Topping the hump in the road, I slow again. Charred ground forms a half circle around the back of the house. On the front porch, in the middle of the wreckage, a little weathered man rocks. A deep breath lights the butterflies afire in my belly. Mr. Wellman stands as my pickup rolls to a stop. I push the door open as he steps down the three steps one at a time. "Good morning, Mr. Wellman." I step toward him. "I'm Nor—"

"Nora Kelly, it's good to finally meet you. Ian has told me a lot about you." He shakes my hand.

My cheeks warm. Ian's been talking about me? But of course he would have been if he gave the lease up for me.

"It's good to meet you too." I stuff my hands in my pockets. "I'm sorry to hear about the fire. It looks like it got up close and personal." A fence post a couple hundred yards from the house is charred.

"It was a little ticklish for a minute there." He studies something beyond me. "Why don't I show you the place?" In a slow but stable gait, he starts toward a broke-in Gator. I follow behind, matching his speed. "Ian hasn't been working you too hard, has he?"

I laugh. "No, if anything the other way around." I watch him slide into the driver's seat and follow suit in the passenger's.

He starts the engine and rests his hand on the gearshift. "This old place has been in my family a long time. Kids don't want it, but I guess now there's not much upkeep to worry about. It's good for the land, though, this fire." He looks over at me. "You ever been in a fire?"

I shake my head. "No, I guess not." Thankfully.

"It'll make your heart flutter." He laughs and shifts to reverse. "Not the way my bride used to make it flutter either."

I laugh with him, mainly because I don't know what else to do.

Carrying us down a well-used trail, the little engine makes it hard to carry on a conversation. When Mr. Wellman gets to the top of a rise that looks over the house, he turns the key off.

Halfway down, a motor-grader has skinned the earth in a circle around the house. That was close. A big oak tree to the side of the carport stands proud, even though the lower branches on the east side are charred.

"And I told my kids I'm not leaving this place. I've lived here too long to leave now." He looks over at me. "This will keep me plenty busy, though, cleaning up here."

For a moment we sit, and I try to think of something to say. He isn't really complaining, just mulling over what could've been. I've done plenty of that myself lately. "Would you like help?"

Eyebrows arched under his straw hat, he waves his hand dismissively. "Those posts get soot everywhere. I'll get it done in time."

I crack a smile. "I'm not afraid of getting dirty." I hop out of the Gator. All but the bottom wire have fallen loose from the nearest post. I put my foot a quarter of the way up the burnt wood and give it a good shove. It falls, leaving me to catch myself.

A chuckle floats from the Gator. "Well, look at you. Throw that in the back of here, if you don't mind."

I do and break off the post behind us. When I move up to the one in front, he moves up and cuts the engine again.

"You know, I never did know your daddy much, but you do remind me a lot of your uncle Ian."

I am glad my back is turned to him, because it is certainly a prideful smile that lights up my face.

"He's always been quiet, but he has so much going on behind them eyes." He laughs. "The first time I worked with him, he wasn't much more than a button. My own kids had gone off to college, but Ian filled most of the gap they left."

I load two more half-eaten posts on top of the others.

"He was a hand, now," Wellman continues. "He was with me on a job for the sheriff's office. We roped a bunch of maverick bulls out of a two-section white brush thicket." He shakes his head. "Man, that was a long day. Several days, actually. Couple of times Ian saved my hide. I made sure not to tell my bride about those until I had been home a few days, then she'd just shake her head." His voice grows soft. "She was good at patching me up."

I catch sight of the shimmering water in his eyes. "How long were y'all married?"

"Sixty-one years. There's not a day goes by that I don't miss her."

I kick another post over. Sixty-one years is a long time to have someone before you have to let them go.

We've gone a mile or so in which I kick the posts out of the ground, Wellman driving up every third post to collect them. He looks back down the way we've come and says, "Dadgum, I've put you to work."

"I don't mind." I grin and dust my hands on my jeans.

"Well, I sure appreciate it." He motions to the seat next to him. "That'll do. Let's go after a drink."

Fewer and fewer charred smells drift on the breeze as we pull back up to the house and I follow him inside. "How long have you had this place?"

He shuffles through the doorway into the kitchen. "Born on this place. My ma and pa managed to hang onto it until I got done gallivanting around and came back."

My lips twitch in a smile as I imagine a young Wellman working around ranches. "It's hard to hold onto a ranch these days." A little sigh I didn't mean to escape me does.

Holding out a glass of tea to me, he motions for me to follow him and turns the corner.

"That's why we've all gotta stick together. Only way we'll keep raising beef." He eases himself into a recliner.

I nod. He's right. We have to stick together and all work for one goal. Raising good beef.

I'll have to swipe Ian's Livestock Weekly *tonight. It's been a bit since I've looked in the classifieds.*

Chapter 17

I lift the T-post driver from the T-post, chest heaving. Sweat soaks the back of my shirt. I wipe my face with my sleeve. Some of the brown dirt stains from my shirt have left. I'm sure my face looks like I've been rolling in dirt now.

Building fence has never been my favorite thing, but it sure beats twiddling my thumbs. After two days piddling around, I practically begged Ian to put me to work.

Leaving the heavy driver against another post, I walk a couple yards to the pickup. I guzzle cool water and cock my hat back. On the other side of my patch work, a couple of cows rummage through greasewood and blackbrush for two sprigs of grass that must be there. I lean up against the pickup. Three days without looking after cattle is probably the longest stint I've done since high school.

Unannounced saltwater claws at my throat, but I swallow it away. I've done enough of that lately.

But what if it isn't so bad? Ian cried, in my very presence. He's seen me cry and didn't disown me.

"You've got to be strong enough to cry."

Anyone who's lost a daughter and kept living is tough. No matter how many tears they cry.

And Wellman, hadn't those been tears in his eyes when he talked about his wife? Not for a moment would I call either of those men weak.

I slide my hat down and grab a roll of stay wire from the bed of the pickup. Even if it isn't a weakness to cry, I don't want to start at it today. Wire in hand, I tie the patch to the stays. My knees whine as I squat to tie the bottom wires. After several miles yesterday and several more today, they're more than upset with me.

Standing again, I look down the wire. The fence makes a straight line toward the highway with the T-posts marking off every ten feet. I breathe in the dust and greasewood air. Dust and greasewood: two things that will always feel like home.

A few hours later, I'm a couple miles down the fence. I see another hole in the fence big enough for a cow to go through. I get the wire stretcher out and attach it to the top wire at two points. The wire is singing tight when I look up at the sound of Ian's silver realtor pickup bouncing over the stumps and rocks and potholes.

"You're making good progress," he says, stepping from the pickup.

I look up at him, the pliers mid twist. "Well, thank you. What are you up to?"

"It's quitting time."

I twist the splice a couple more times on each end before letting the stretcher loose. "There's still daylight." I smile at his chuckle.

He hands me a piece of stay wire and takes the fence stretcher from me. "Do you enjoy this?"

I look over my shoulder with one cocked eyebrow. "Oh, definitely." The words drip with sarcasm. I shrug my shoulders. "Really, though, it's not bad, especially when there's nothing better to do and no rush."

"What if there was something better to do?"

I glance over my shoulder again. What's he up to? There isn't a teasing tone in his voice. I finish tying the wire to the T-post. He hands me another piece of wire before walking past me. Okay...?

When he comes back, he has a roll of papers in his hand. "Come here."

I slide the pliers into my back pocket and look over his arm as he spreads the papers out among the fencing tools.

"Do you remember these?"

Maps. Dotted lines for fences and circles for water troughs. "These are some of the leases you pulled up for Wade, over by Big Lake."

Ian's face is like a ray of sunshine. "Exactly! A buddy of mine has them contracted on a five-year lease." He looks into my eyes. "And he needs someone to run his operation."

My eyebrows reach for my hairline. They ask the question my voice can't seem to.

"He has a couple truckloads of pairs unloading in two weeks. I know they aren't heifers and there won't be as many of them, but if you want the job, it's yours."

My lips spread wide before I bite the bottom one. "Really?"

He smiles one to match mine. "There's even a nice little house."

I wouldn't care if the house has mice. "Thank you," I say, throwing my arms around him and squeezing tight.

***

Rolling up the door of the storage unit puts a smile on my face. It doesn't get to hold my things for long. James and Ian already helped me move most of my stuff; only three big boxes sit inside the door now. I wrap my arms around the top one and start toward the pickup.

I push the first box into the bed until it hits the gooseneck ball. The last two easily sit side by side just inside the tailgate. I shut it and grab the combination lock from the storage unit latch. Just before sliding into the driver's seat, I drop the lock in the pocket inside the door. The trilling of my phone hits my ears as soon as the door slams behind me.

Dad.

I take a deep breath and blow it out. "Hello."

"Hey, is it hot enough for you?"

On cue I roll the window down. "Just a little bit." I start the engine and look both ways before pulling out onto the street.

"Well, did you get everything moved?"

I stop myself from laughing out loud. After all, I am the one that told them they didn't need to help. "Taking the last boxes out right now. Cattle will be in next week."

A door clicks on his end of the line. "Well, that's good." He pauses. "You'll have more fun there than at Dan's office."

A smile barely lifts my lips. "Yeah." *Thanks for admitting that.* I make the turn into the post office parking lot. "How's Mom?"

"She's good! She's got her garden blooming."

I nod as if it will drive the conversation forward. "That's good." I drum my fingers against the steering wheel. We already talked about the weather, Mom, and that I'm moved. I've run out of topics.

Dad's rhythmic breathing keeps time through the line for several moments. Then he clears his throat. "You have everything you need for the new house?"

I put the pickup in park and lean against the door. "I think so. It's about the same size as the other one."

"Good, good."

I can see his signature head bob, and my lips twitch into a little smile.

"Well, I'm about to lose service. I'll holler at y'all later. Love you!"

I press my hat on my head and grip the door handle. "All right, Dad. Love you too."

"Bye."

Stepping down onto the concrete, my shoulders are square and my steps feel lighter. It is all out on the table now. I'm not folding to a desk job, and Dad has recognized that, though not in so many words.

There is a small stack of mail in my box, but I don't look at it until I'm pulled up in front of the cream-colored house. Before putting the pickup in park, I run over a few dried cow patties.

Yep, this is home.

I flip past bills and junk mail, but a card-sized envelope stops me. I slit the top open with my pocketknife and pull out a little piece of lined paper.

Nora,

Thank you for your help and the visit. Come back anytime. And don't be afraid to sit in the feelings. You'll get a lot of them on a ranch.

Wellman.

Chapter 18

3:15.

I stare at the bright red block letters on the alarm clock by my bed. Rolling away from the clock, I let a sigh out. It has barely been an hour since I last looked at it. Two truckloads of cattle will arrive in about five hours and it would be real nice to be rested for that. Excitement mixed with anxiety won't let me get much sleep, though.

Flopping over on my back, I stare up at the popcorn ceiling. I already got the hay put out in water lots and spent the last week making sure the fences were up. Everything is ready for the pairs, and James will be over shortly to help me process them. If I had to guess, I'd say Ian is just a little jealous that we get to play with cattle and he has to show a ranch today.

I doze off for another hour before getting out of bed. A cup of coffee is ready in a few minutes, and I curl up with it in my brown chair. Gazing out the window, I watch the mesquite leaves flutter in front of the bright moon and lift my mug to my lips.

After a couple sips, I pull my Bible from the table by my chair and lay it open in my lap. My bookmark rests in Proverbs sixteen. I read slowly, sipping on my coffee every couple verses. Verse nine catches my attention, and I read it over again, out loud this time. "In his heart, a man plans his course, but the Lord determines his path."

A little smile lifts my lips. Ain't that the truth. I sure didn't plan to end up in Big Lake, Texas' backyard, but here I am. And pretty darn excited about it too.

Thank you, Lord, for determining my path.

After I finish reading, I slip into my jeans and plaid shirt for the day. In my worn-out Nikes, I stroll out to the pens. The white on Banks' and Cante's faces shines in the moonlight. "Good morning, boys," I call, as I veer to the right into the barn.

Armed with a bucket full of feed, I slip through the gate into their pen. Each of them cautiously stretches his nose towards the bucket. "Patience." I switch arms with it and shoo them away. I split the feed into three troughs and slip back out the gate.

With the horses fed, I rummage around in the fridge until I find a couple slices of bacon and the last few eggs I have. They ought to make for a filling breakfast.

While they crackle in skillets, I slip to my closet and grab my boots with the spurs already strapped on them. My spurs jingle as I speed-walk through the living room back to the kitchen trying to stir the eggs before they burn too badly. Half of them have already stuck to the bottom in a thick layer.

That's all right. I didn't need that much food, anyway.

I reach up and flip the knob off for the burner under the bacon and then rake the eggs from the skillet onto a plate. Behind me, the unmistakable squeak of the door hinges sounds. I jerk around to face the door, skillet in hand and my eyebrows scrunched together.

"Well, look at that! I did make it in time for breakfast."

"James! Dadgummit, I was ready to smack you with this thing." I put the skillet on a hot pad and glance at the time. "You're a little early, aren't you?"

His spurs ring with his nearing steps. "Well, I had to get fuel this morning, and I didn't know what mood that construction stoplight would be in, so I left plenty early." He chuckles and pulls out a chair. "Turns out the stoplight didn't take long at all."

I shake my head with a chuckle. "Well, I burned half of it, but you are welcome to some breakfast."

"I already ate. Thank you, though."

"Coffee?"

He smiles and rises from the dining room chair. "Sure, that'd be good."

I grab a mug and fill it before handing it to him.

"Thank you, ma'am."

"You're welcome." I turn back to the stove and throw a tortilla on the griddle. "Thanks for helping me today."

His coffee cup clinks on the table. "Heck yeah! Glad I could. This is a nice place."

I nod. "I think it will be with a little polishing up." Tortilla done, I flop it on my plate, line it with eggs, and lay the bacon on top. I sit in the chair across from James with a topped-off coffee cup. "How have you been?"

James takes a sip of his coffee and sets the mug on the table. A little sigh leaves his parted lips. "All right, I guess."

I raise my eyebrows, encouraging him to continue, and take another bite.

"My family has been a bit of a mess lately. My sister lost her baby." He pushes a heavy breath out. "Was supposed to be the first grandbaby and all that."

The food in my mouth instantly turns dry. And he's here helping me? Hurrying to chew my food, I try to think of something to say. "I'm sorry, James, that's so hard." I wash the burrito down with coffee.

"Thanks." His voice breaks, and he quickly lifts his coffee mug to his lips.

I start to reach across the table, but I can't reach his hand and pull mine back. "Sometimes tears are the only accurate way to express what we feel inside. I guess God made it like that for a reason."

"Maybe so." He meets my eyes, and I don't look away. In a couple seconds he moves his gaze to his boots and shuffles them. "So how are you settling in out here?"

I shrug one shoulder, the last bite of my burrito pinched between my fingers. "Pretty good. It'll feel more like home once we unload the trucks."

He shakes his head. "Dangit, Nora, I'm really sorry. I wished I could have changed how things ended up with Wade."

"Thanks, but it's okay. It's not been all a joyride, but things have turned out like they were meant to."

"I don't know how you've been so okay with how all this unfolded."

A little chuckle floats from my lips. "Oh, I've had my fair share of fits over it. But even the sadness has taught me a thing or two."

James smiles, and I suddenly feel like I stuck my foot in my mouth. He *just* told me his family was facing a hard time. I drain the last of my coffee and put the mug on top of my plate, taking them to the sink. After rinsing the dishes, I pull the towel from the stove handle and dry my hands. The time takes a second to register in my head. "Is it really already seven?"

Checking the time on his phone, James nods. "Looks like it."

I throw the towel on the counter beside the sink. "I guess I better get in gear then. I still need to saddle a pony." Planting myself back in my chair at the table, I reach for one of my boots and turn it upside down. A mesquite leaf flutters out. I slide my foot in and reach for the other one.

James rinses his coffee mug out and is waiting by the door for me when I put my hat on my head. "My lady," he says and swings the door open.

I giggle. "Thank you."

For a couple paces, James walks beside me. Then he slows down, slipping to my other side. "I'll go ahead and unload. Where should I park to be out of the way?"

"You can pull up in front of the house."

"On top of all your grass?" James tosses the words over his shoulder, already veering off to his pickup.

I laugh. "All forty sprigs of it." I'm still several yards away from the pens when one of my geldings nickers softly. "You missed me already?"

From the peg inside the barn, I pull my hackamore and head for the pen. All three geldings lope a couple circles around the pen before settling down in the corner. I ease up amongst them. Cante's muscles are tight as I rub my hand down his neck and slip the reins around. "Your time to shine, bud." I slip the bosal over his nose.

Atop his horse, James sits at the gate. "Breaking in the youngin, huh?"

I shrug. "I figure there won't be anyone waiting on us, so it'll be a good time to make him do pen work."

James nods. "Darn right."

I start to lead Cante off, and James clears his throat. Stopping, I half turn to see him over the sorrel's back.

"Do you want me to set these gates up while you saddle him?"

"Ah, sure." I turn Cante around and stand beside James' mount. "If you want to make it a straight shot out to the water lot with hay in it. I think we'll send them out there and then bring them back to process them once everything is unloaded."

He nods. "Sounds good."

"Thank you!"

I saddle Cante and trot him around in a couple circles before swinging into the saddle. Being as all we have left to do is wait for the trucks, I ride into the water lot and trot figure eights.

At eight on the dot, two cattle trucks come down the road in a cloud of dust. I think of the last cloud of dust I saw cattle trucks in, but this time headlights are pointed my way instead of taillights. My heart does a dance like a butterfly in my chest, and a grin takes over my lips.

James guides the driver back to the chute. Within moments the scraping of hooves on the truck floor fills the air, mixed with the bawling of mommas looking for their babies. Occasionally, Cante and I ride out of our spot in the corner to push cows down the alley and make room for the next ones.

The second truck replaces the first at the chute. Several more compartmentfuls of cows spill from it, before it changes to little red bald-faced calves. As they throw their tails up and jump off the cement chute, landing on dirt, my cheeks start to hurt because I'm smiling so wide.

Within fifteen minutes, the second truck is empty, and I wave to the drivers. "Thank you!" I holler over the uproar of cows calling for their calves.

James rides up beside me, his smile wide too. "Well, what do you think of them?"

A little squeak escapes my lips. I lean down and rub a hand on each side of Cante's neck. "They're perfect! I just want to squeeze the little calves."

With a chuckle and a shake of his head, James says, "You're one of the only people I know that will look at a bunch of half-skeleton Herefords and tell me you think they're perfect."

I shrug. "They have more flesh than those we shipped off Wade's. Besides, they're perfect, because, at least for now, God has given me the chance to look after them."

A moment of silence passes before I look over at James to find him watching me. A blush heats my cheeks. "What?"

"You just haven't smiled like that in a while." He ducks his head and repositions his hand on his reins. "What all are we doing to these guys?"

"There's three or four shots for the cows, need to brand them, and worm them. Then just mark the calves like usual." I nudge Cante forward. "Don't you think we ought to let them sit for just a little while longer, though?"

James shrugs. "Sure thing. You're the boss lady."

I laugh. "I'm going to look at them. Are you coming?" I ride off and hear his horse's steps behind me.

Cante's slow steps through the herd barely disturb them. My head swivels from side to side as I look over each cow. They aren't some east Texas Herefords. These girls have hooves half the size of dinner plates and bones bigger around than the pipe the pens are made of. They'll do just fine out here.

We make it around the herd to the gate out of the water lot. I sidle Cante up to it and pull the handle up. Before pulling the gate open, I draw in a deep breath. The smells of cow patties, caliche, and greasewood mix and fill my lungs. A satisfied smile perks my lips.

That's the smell of home.

Bonus Scene

Are you still wrapped up in Nora's world? You don't have to leave yet!

Get a scene from this book, but from Ian's point of view!

Just go to sequoyahbranham.com/afteritcoc to download your bonus scene.

Glossary

Leggins

Leather pants, minus the seat, that protect the cowboy(girl)'s legs from brush and weather elements.

Pickin' string

A short piece of rope, usually carried on one's saddle and leggins. It is a universal tool, being used to tie gates close, to tie down a wayward calf, or as a dog leash.

Latigo

A long leather strap on a saddle used to adjust the cinch.

Dally

Referring to when a cowboy wraps his rope around the saddle horse to hold.

Cake

Feed high in protein and shaped into cubes for cattle.

Hackamore

Headgear to ride a horse in that does not have a bit. Instead, it has a noseband called a **Bosal**.

Nylon Deficiency

A slang term cowboys will say when referring to a cow that will not corporate and must be roped to be brought into the pen.

Billet

A piece of leather or nylon on either side of the saddle to hold the cinch in place. In Nora's case, used only for the back cinch.

Acknowledgements

Where do I start? There are so many people who have been through this journey. It's not been without its highs and lows. Thank you to all that have been there along the way.

Madeline, my ride or die, my cheerleader, my shoulder, my crutch—I could go on. You've been there for it all and kept me going through times I wouldn't have made it through without you. I wouldn't have made it through writing this book, the rounds of edits, and the incredibly long checklists if it weren't for you.

Brett Harris and Kara Swanson, the dynamic duo that makes the best coaches on the planet. Every day you make dreams come true for writers like me. The best part, though, is that you don't do the leg work for us. You build the obstacle course and give us a map and cheer us on and challenge us as we build our own muscles. Thank you for the hard work the two of you have put in to help me get this far.

Juliet, my buddy. Somewhere along this journey we linked arms, and you've been a staple in my life since! I can't thank you enough for the hours of brainstorming and all the many phone calls to talk about all the feelings. Thank you for loving this story as much as I do and always rooting for it. Thank you for being such an amazing example of cheering someone on while waiting to get to enjoy that same achievement yourself. You may be younger than me in years, but each and every time I talk to you I learn so much.

Juliet, Josiah, and Jadyn, thank you for being the first people to read this story and so thoughtfully critique it. You helped me grow it so much, and I can't thank you enough.

Lauren Hildebrand, the best editor in the world! Again, you saw this story as just a fledgling novella and gave it so much love. You challenged me to rewrite it all over again, but also fangirled about a line or two. (Pretty sure my co-workers thought I was crazy as I yelled "I knew that was a good line!" while reading my edit letter.) Thank you!

Joanne, you have walked with me in creating this novella each step of the way. From the very first time you saw this concept, you handled it—and me—with so much love and care. I can't thank you enough for nurturing not only this story, but also myself.

Annie, my line editor. You didn't just contribute to this project, you contributed to my heart. You were so thoughtful to take time beyond your editing comments and point out some of your favorite parts of this story. One of those comments made one of my writer-dreams come true before this book was ever printed. Thank you!

Kellyn Roth, you'll never admit it, but I'm sure there was at least one time you wished I wouldn't bring all my many questions to you. Thank you for taking the time to share all of your indie publishing tips with me! You're the big sister in publishing that I didn't even know I needed.

I want to thank everyone at The Author Conservatory. Brett and Kara may have founded this amazing program, but it takes every single one of you to keep it going. Each of the students from the community— I cannot thank you enough for cheering me on and helping me get this book out in the world. Y'all are truly the best community I could ask for!

Did you love *In The Company Of Cows*? Then you should read *In Between Pastures*[1] by Sequoyah Branham!

For the first time in her twenty-two years, Nora Kelly is finding fulfillment in more than just tending cattle. Joining the local horse club and discussing life with her Uncle Ian have brought new light to her life.

Everything is going great until Ian goes to the ER and Nora's bright new world is wrecked by two words. It's cancer.

Checking fence turns into checking on Ian in the hospital. Rides on Nora's Colt turn to miles in the old pickup back and forth from her house to Ian's tending both sets of cattle.

1. https://books2read.com/u/mK8ep9

2. https://books2read.com/u/mK8ep9

Nora just wants to be as much support to Ian as he has been to her in the past. But the harder she tries to keep everything running the more things fall apart. When James, her old coworker, tries to help, she pushes him away. For how can she accept help without becoming a failure to her uncle, the strongest man she's ever known?

When—for the first time—Nora admits Ian might not make it she's forced to consider if ranch chores is the best way to help him. Are the plates she's trying to keep spinning actually pulling her away from the most important thing? Does she have enough time to show her love to Ian before it's too late?

About the Author

Sequoyah Branham is passionate about sharing the beauty and heartbreak of ranching. Working on ranches across Texas gives her a wide variety of experiences to draw inspiration from for her characters and the obstacles they face. She enjoys long days in the saddle with good friends and her dog by her side as often as she can.

Catch up with her on her website www.sequoyahbranham.com